ONE
RIDE

A HOLLYWOOD CHRONICLES NOVEL

A.L. JACKSON & REBECCA SHEA

A.L. Jackson
www.aljacksonauthor.com
Rebecca Shea
www.rebeccasheaauthor.com
Cover Design by RBA Designs
Editing by AW Editing
Formatting by Mesquite Business Services

Print ISBN: 978-1-946420-23-7
eBook ISBN: 978-1-946420-24-4

ONE WILD RIDE

one

Elle

I tossed the garment bag onto the backseat of my car, balancing my phone between my ear and shoulder as I maneuvered my huge bag into the front passenger seat. "I'm heading back to my place right now. Don't worry. I'll be there."

"I swear, if you're late, I'm going to skin you alive." Leave it to Kay-Kay to get all spun up and agitated.

"Oh, come on, Kay-Kay. You've been crushing on Paxton Myles since the day I met you. Don't act like you aren't salivating to get to that theater. Besides, have I ever let you down?" I asked her.

Kaylee Rose Burton hesitated on the other end of the line as if she didn't know how to answer that question. "No, you haven't. And for the record, I so don't have a crush on Paxton Myles. He's *famous.*"

She whispered *famous* as if it was some massive secret, which it so was not since Paxton Myles was indeed famous.

Very famous.

It was why I basically had to force her into agreeing to come.

She'd been my best friend since we'd been paired together as roommates at UCLA as freshman. An unlikely match, that was for sure.

She was about as conservative as they came, and I'd been voted the biggest partier in my high school. Honestly, at the time, I'd been a little horrified that my parents were actually making me live in a dorm. With a stranger, nonetheless.

Ten years later, I could look back and totally understand what they were trying to do and fully appreciated them for it. Tossing me out of my privileged nest, praying I'd spread my wings, flap them hard and fast, and maybe just soar.

Make it out in the real world by myself.

The last thing I wanted to be was some spoiled brat living off her daddy's dime for her whole life.

No, thank you.

But that sure didn't mean my daddy wasn't my world. And tonight was his *big* night. It wasn't just that I'd be letting Kaylee down. More importantly, I'd be letting him down, too, and that was just not going to happen. "I will be there," I told her, slamming my door shut and pressing the button to start the ignition of my car. "I'll call you when I'm getting close."

"Okay, drive safe," Kaylee told me.

"I always do." I ended the call, dropped my cell into the center console, and shifted my car into reverse as I mentally went through my list of things I needed to do.

Hair, nails, and makeup?

Check, check, check.

All thanks to Gregorio, who'd had me in his chair for basically the whole day.

Dress?

I peeked in the rearview mirror into the backseat at the garment bag I'd just laid across the seat.

Huge check.

I bit back a squeal.

I couldn't wait to get back to my condo to slip out of my VS sweatpants and tank and into the gorgeousness.

All I had to do was rush back across town, change, and climb into the limo.

I glanced down at the time on the dash.

Oh, you know, all in about under five minutes.

Shit.

A pulse of anxiety thrummed in my chest, and I took a deep breath and pasted on a smile.

No worries.

I had this.

I always did.

I started to back out of the parking spot when my eye snagged on the billboard across the street.

My daddy had always told me I had the attention span of a two-year-old.

I begged to differ.

It was my attention getting fixated on something that usually got me into trouble. So distracted and wrapped up that I didn't have the first clue what was going on around me except for that singular focus.

Take this billboard, for instance.

I blamed it on the marketing degree I had tucked under my belt as well as everything I'd learned at the ad company where I'd worked for the last five years.

It was all due to that keen, savvy eye.

I couldn't help but stare at the advertisement for an upscale shop on Rodeo Drive.

Plastered on that billboard was what had to be the sexiest man I'd ever seen. He was in nothing but a pair of tight black underwear, his arms folded over his head, a pose that showcased the most glorious set of abs a woman could ever hope to imagine existed outside the realm of Photoshop.

Too bad I knew that all that ridiculous muscle had to have been fabricated on the screen.

The thing was, though, the smolder on his face was enough to ignite a fire.

One right in the center of me, and I was pretty sure that was not something that could be forged.

Obviously, a display of clothes wasn't necessary to sell them.

Beauty always captured the eye. Sex sold it.

It was only natural.

It was simply human nature to be drawn to it.

So what harm could a little ogling of a picture do? Especially considering every man I came across in this city turned out to be nothing but a douchebag doing anything it took to make it in Hollywood.

I'd settled on a look, but don't touch policy.

I never felt guilty about doing a little admiring, especially knowing I could bank it for future reference.

You know, for the job.

The text coming in on my phone alerting me that my driver was already waiting at my condo shocked me out of my trance.

Apparently, I'd been *looking* a little too long.

Crap, I really was going to be late for the premier of my father's first A-list movie he'd directed.

The payoff of all his hard work.

And I'd be sitting in the front row with him to celebrate that achievement.

I pressed down on the accelerator to back out of the parking spot.

Crunch.

That was all I heard, this horrible grating and grinding and scraping that pierced my ears as my car jostled and jerked.

I rammed on the breaks, my gaze flying to the rearview mirror to see what I'd hit.

Nothing.

There was nothing there, but I knew it had to be something.

Heart stampeding in my chest, I put my car into park, tentative as I unlatched the door, not quite sure what it was I was going to find, praying it wasn't something bad.

I stepped out, my breaths going short as I edged around to the back of my car, first seeing a wheel, then metal.

More metal.

A motorcycle.

Oh, shit.

A motorcycle.

Panic thundered through my being as I inched forward, the breath fully leaving my lungs when a man came into view, lying right behind my car on his back and writhing in pain.

"Oh my God, are you okay?" I rushed, flying over to his side, dropping to my knees on the pitted pavement.

I scoured him for injuries, but I couldn't see anything since he was completely covered by a helmet and a leather jacket and holey jeans. The problem was that I wasn't sure if they'd started out that way or not.

But there was no blood, and I was taking that as a good sign.

His fingers fumbled with the helmet clasp under his jaw, and he ripped it off, gasping for air.

Holy shit.

Holy shit.

My mouth dropped open.

He peeled a single eye open and stared up at me. "Am I dead?"

I blinked at him, his deep voice shocking me out of my stupor, my words falling fast from my tongue. "What? No, you aren't dead. Why are you asking that? Are you hurt? Oh God, tell me you aren't really hurt," I begged.

He squinted up through the sunlight that poured down around his ridiculously gorgeous face.

For the love of God, what was wrong with me that I was noticing that?

"Because you're looking at me like you've seen a ghost."

I laughed.

Outright laughed.

I blamed it on the adrenaline rush.

"Maybe I have," I told him, glancing between his face staring up at the sky and the one that was oozing sex from the billboard.

Yep.

Same guy.

I'd just run over the hottest guy on earth.

Of course, I had.

Just my luck.

He groaned, and I gasped. "Are you hurt?"

"What does it look like, Princess? I just got mowed down with a BMW. I think my ankle's broken."

"Oh God."

"I usually like to hear that under different circumstances. Why don't we try again when I'm not so . . . incapacitated?"

My eyes narrowed. "Are you coming on to me right now?"

"Did you just run me over right now?" he shot back.

Shit.

I had.

"Please just tell me my baby is okay."

Panic surged through my blood. "Your baby?"

A chuckle rumbled from his chest. "My bike. My baby. But if you want to take that title, I'll gladly oblige."

This guy.

He started to sit up, and I set my hand on his shoulder. "Maybe you shouldn't move. Let me call an ambulance."

He gave a harsh shake of his head and pushed up to sitting, running a palm over the top of his cropped dark hair. "No. It's just my ankle. You can take me."

My eyes went wide. "What?"

He looked at me with those eyes, black as obsidian. "You did just run me over. I would think you could do me the courtesy of getting me to the emergency room."

"I-I-I—"

Crap.

I looked between him and his bike and my car, realizing how quickly time was slipping away.

I really was going to be late.

"Help me up so we can move my bike."

I hesitated for a second.

He caught it. "Are you really worried about getting your hands a little dirty, Princess?"

He drew Princess out like it was a vulgar word.

Pushing to standing, I huffed and extended my hand to help him. "No. I just haven't done anything like this before."

"What? Run a man over?"

A scoff bled free. "Funny, I was talking about handling a motorcycle."

His gaze swept me, head to toe. "Oh, I'm sure you handle things just fine."

My mouth dropped open.

Speechless.

Flattered or offended, I couldn't decide.

He reached out and took the hand that I had extended.

The second his skin met mine, quivers of heat streaked up my arm.

Oh God. He really did have the power to set me on fire.

He wobbled as he tried to balance on one foot.

"Are you good?" I asked, trying to pretend I wasn't totally affected by his presence.

Look, don't touch.

Look, don't touch.

"I think I am now, considering an angel was sent to save me."

"The flattery," I tossed at him.

He grinned.

Dimples lighting on both sides of his cheeks.

Oh damn.

"Come on, let's get your bike out of the way and get you to the hospital. I have somewhere I have to be in an hour."

"You're seriously going to ditch me when you just ran me down?"

"I'm not ditching you. It's just . . . important."

His eyes narrowed, taking me in, my hair and makeup done while I stood there in a pair of old sweats, as if he was trying to add up me up, figure it out. "And what is so important?"

My mind flashed to the fact he was on a billboard. His striking face. The fact he was here, in Hollywood.

Where all the guys were the same.

I bit back the explanation because I sure didn't want to give him any details about where I was headed tonight.

Mischief swam through his expression. "You broke my ankle, Princess. I could have died. Tell me you didn't risk my life to take a selfie for an Instagram post."

Says the guy who's bleeding sex on the billboard behind him.

I didn't say it.

Pretended I didn't see it. That I didn't know he was probably just like every guy desperate to make it in L.A.

"Get in the car," I told him. "I wouldn't want you to die on me."

There was no keeping the sarcasm from the words.

Because this guy was most definitely killing me.

two

Kassius

"What the hell are you doing?" I yell as she weaves carelessly in and out of L.A. traffic like it's her job. All the zig-zagging and sharp turns has me growling in pain. No wonder she ran me over, she drives like a damn maniac.

"Getting you to the hospital," she bites, chancing a quick glance at me before switching lanes back again.

This girl is stunning. Stunning actually doesn't even describe her beauty. Tall and lean with light olive skin, dark hair, and brown eyes. She's a living, breathing angel . . . with a sassy mouth that doesn't stop.

"I can't believe I ran over a model," she mumbles as if she's talking to herself, her perfectly manicured thumbs tapping each side of the steering wheel, which she currently has a death grip on. "An underwear model. I fucking hit a hot underwear model." Another mumble and some more tapping and another lane switch. "Kay-Kay is never going to believe this."

"I'm right here, I can hear you, you know?"

"Shut up!" She yanks the wheel to the right, hard, and we do another aggressive lane change, this time, barely slipping into the space between two cars.

"Are you trying to kill me?" I yell as she jams on the breaks to avoid eating the ass end of the car in front of us. "Because I feel like maybe you want to finish me off."

She looks at me and rolls her eyes. "No, but I really do have somewhere to be and taking you to the hospital wasn't in my plans."

Her eyes dart to the clock display on her dash.

"And you nearly killing me really wasn't in *my* plans today, but I really need to get this ankle looked at, Princess."

"I didn't try to kill you."

"Depends how you look at it."

She lets out a deep sigh, as if she's resigning herself to the fact that she did damn near kill me. "What's your name?" she finally asks when we hit a red light. I release a deep breath from my lungs.

"Kassius. You can call me Kas. You?"

"Elle."

Elle. Fucking beautiful Elle with big brown eyes and a touch of pink on her cheeks and perfectly plump lips. Lips I'd love to have wrapped around my—

"Kas." Elle snaps me out of my filthy thoughts. "I'm going to pull up to the doors at the ER. There should be someone there to help you with a wheel chair." I look at her as she tucks a piece of her dark hair behind her ear.

"You aren't coming in with me? Maybe we can you find a sexy candy striper uniform—"

"Gross." She kills my dream with one word. "Where's your phone?"

"Where are your manners?"

"I don't have any, now get me your damn phone." I love it that she's bossy. That smart little mouth of hers purses as she waits for me to pull the sleek phone from the pocket of my leather jacket.

"Here." I shake it in front of her, and she snatches it from my hands and starts pounding on the screen before handing it back to me.

"You really should have a passcode on your phone." This woman has the audacity to bust my nuts over not having a passcode on my phone when she damn near killed me fifteen minutes ago.

Elle hands my phone back to me. "My number is in there. I'll cover any medical bills and any damage to your *baby*." The stoplight turns green, and she takes off, yanking the steering wheel hard to the left again as we turn toward the entrance for the hospital ER.

"Sorry to up and leave you like this, but I really have to go." She glances at the clock display again. "Fuck," she mumbles under her breath and presses a hand to her forehead as if she's feeling for a fever. "I'm never going to make it."

I smile at this crazy woman as she talks to herself. As we pull under the porte cochere, Elle waves her hands excitedly, flagging down a gentleman with a wheel chair.

Rolling down her window she yells, "He needs a wheelchair," and points to the passenger seat directing them to me. The gentleman wearing scrubs opens my door and eases the wheelchair into place so that I should be able to lift myself from the car seat and fall into the wheelchair almost effortlessly.

"It was a pleasure hitting you, Kas!" Elle says, her lips twisting into a mischievous smile.

"It wasn't a pleasure being hit by you, Elle!" I holler back just as the car door slams closed. She rolls down the passenger window and leans over the passenger seat.

"Send me the bills!" It's the last thing she says before offering a wave of her hand and taking off out of the lot, her silver BMW tires screeching as she speeds away.

"What was that?" the guy pushing me through the sliding glass doors asks.

"Everything I think I've ever wanted," I respond, a smile pulling at my lips.

"Mr. Cowen," the older doctor says as he pulls up a set of X-rays on his laptop. "It's definitely broken." He points to the black-and-white picture that shows my right ankle with a broken bone. "The good news is, it's a clean break. We'll get you in a temporary splint until your swelling goes down and then we'll need to cast it.

You'll be non-weight bearing for four to eight weeks."

Four to eight weeks? Holy shit. Dominic, my agent, was so not gonna be kosher with that. If I thought Elle was busting my nuts . . .

"The bad news is that you were hit by a car, and although you were wearing a helmet, you're showing signs of a concussion. We'd like you to stay overnight for observation."

"Observation? I was wearing a helmet and the only thing that hurts is my ankle," I argue with him.

"Do I need to remind you again that you were hit by a car?" He looks at me over the top of his wire-rimmed glasses. "I'd like to do a CT scan to make sure there is no internal damage. If that checks out clear, you can go home tomorrow."

The old man stands, sliding the laptop under his arm as he looks down at me. "Someone from registration will be by shortly and we'll get that ankle splinted after your CT scan."

I clench my jaw and nod, dismissing the doctor. "Who would you like us to notify of your admission?"

Fucking Elle . . . silver-BMW-driving princess, that was who.

"Let me get you a number." I smirk, and he nods before sauntering away.

three

Elle

My limo left me, the zipper on my dress got caught on a red sequin, and the curls ironed into my hair were falling out of their hold.

But I was going to make it on time, damn it.

I was going to make it.

Stumbling into the elevator in my heels and trying not to trip over the short train at the back of my dress, I anxiously poked at the garage floor button.

"Come on, come on, come on," I coaxed as the elevator swiftly dropped from the top penthouse floor where my condo was located to the parking garage in the basement.

The second the doors slid open, I was racing for my car that now had a big scrape across the back bumper.

Compliments of one Kas Cowen.

Obviously, the memory of him wasn't going to be erased quite so easily.

Pushing down the jolt of remorse that just had to be mixed with a fat dose of attraction, I focused on getting to my dad's premier. An hour ago, Kaylee had texted me that her limo was picking her up and she'd see me there, which she damned well would.

I jerked my car out of its spot—albeit a little more carefully than I'd done earlier this afternoon. For the first time, I wished that maybe I had traded my *baby* in earlier this year like I'd considered before I'd decided to save a little more for a down payment.

My parents had gotten me this car as a high school graduation present and my condo for my college graduation.

Both over the top and ostentatious and done with the biggest amount of love and care that I ever could have imagined. It also would have been stupid of me to refuse either under the guise of wanting to stand on my own two feet.

I wasn't so spoiled that I didn't recognize that.

Now, I was determined to do the rest by myself.

But, damn, had I splurged and purchased a new car a little earlier, I might actually have had a backup camera like every other normal human being on the face of the planet seemed to. Had I, I wouldn't have run Kas down.

God only knew how much that accident was going to cost me.

Hell, I'd be lucky if that man didn't sue me.

I jumped out into the heavy evening traffic, cursing under my breath. Luckily, the theater should only be about ten minutes away.

My phone rang from the console. It had to be Kaylee wondering where I was. Again.

I reached for it to assure her I was just around the corner, freezing up when I saw the name on the screen.

It was the same hospital I'd dropped Kas off earlier.

Panic surged through me.

What if he was hurt worse than just a broken ankle? What if something horrible happened between the time I'd left him at the door and now? Maybe I should have gone in with him. Made sure he was okay.

Warily, I answered it. "Hello?"

"Ms. Elle?" a woman asked from the other end of the line.

Ms. Elle.

I bit back a laugh. I hadn't even given him my last name. Some things you just had to protect.

"Yes?"

"Hi, I'm Martha in admitting at St. John's. We have your number listed as the next of kin for Mr. Kassius Cowen."

Next of kin?

"Is he . . . okay?" I managed.

"He does have a broken ankle, and we are keeping him for monitoring, but we do need you to come in and sign some paperwork in order for us to admit him and get him to imaging for a CT scan."

"Sign paperwork?"

"You are listed as the guarantor."

Shit. I'd told him I would pay for whatever was needed. And I would. But I needed to get to that premier. "Is that . . . necessary?"

"The ER physician wants to ensure he doesn't have a concussion. He was hit by a car. And he's asking for you." Was that a little sarcasm in her voice?

God, I had to be the most selfish person in the world. This guy could actually be injured. Really injured. Even if he was a huge pain in my ass and got under my skin in the flash of a second I didn't know if I could just leave him hanging like this.

But just being in his presence felt dangerous.

And exciting.

Bad Elle, I scolded myself. *Look, don't touch.* But, somehow, I knew even looking at this man could get me in to trouble.

But this wasn't about me.

This was about a guy I'd mowed down with me car and my father's premier. No matter which choice I made, I was going to be letting someone down.

And I wanted to be there for my father. I did. More than anything. But Kas was relying on me for his well-being. His health had to win out.

I jerked into the next lane and made a quick right turn. "I'll be there in five minutes," I told her and killed the call, gunning the engine as I headed toward the hospital. I weaved in and out of traffic, making quick turns, and what felt like a moment later, I was swinging into a parking spot and running into the ER in a red-sequined dress.

People staring.

Just awesome.

I ran to the counter and asked for Kas. Two minutes later, I was being led down a hall and into a curtained-off area, the admitting nurse telling me she would be bringing in the paperwork for me to sign.

"Thank you," I told her as I pushed aside the drape to step into the small space.

My breath left me.

Kas was lying in the bed, his jacket and clothing traded for a hospital gown.

The goofiest grin on his face. "Princess," he said, slurring a little.

I frowned. "Kas?"

"What are you wearing? I really must be dead. Women just don't really look like that in real life. Come here, angel, get in this bed with me."

Redness flew across my flesh, deep enough I'm sure it matched my gown. "Are you drunk?" I asked him.

A deep chuckle rumbled out, and he swung his arm around that was attached to a tube. "Nope. But I am feeling jussstttt fine," he drew out, slurring on the last. Clearly, they had something potent dripping into his veins.

"You were in pain?" I cringed when I said it, the realization that I had actually *hit* a man today finally settling in.

He lifted one eyebrow. "Broken ankle, Princess. That shit hurts."

"I'm really sorry." I meant it.

His mouth quirked up on one side. "Don't worry yourself. I'm sure you can make it up to me."

"Not gonna happen," I told him, not even close to missing his suggestion, before I waved my phone toward him. "I need to make a call."

"Make it fast. I don't like to be alone. I might get . . . scared."

I didn't even try to keep from rolling my eyes at him.

This guy was too much.

I stepped outside his curtained-off room, having a hard time believing I'd let the man goad me into not leaving him because he didn't want to be alone.

Talk about a guilt trip.

But that was how I felt.

Guilty.

I dialed Kaylee's number. I knew the second she answered that I was in trouble.

"Where are you?"

I pushed out a breath. "I'm so sorry, Kay-Kay, but something came up."

"Something came up?" she screeched.

Yep. There it was. More guilt.

"I know you don't understand right now, and I'll explain it later, but right now I just need you to be there for my daddy on his big day."

"Oh no . . . .no . . . no way am I going there without you."

"Please, Kaylee," I begged desperately. "I already hate that I'm doing this to Daddy. Both of us can't not show. He'll be devastated." I peeked over my shoulder where they were getting ready to move Kas to his private room. "And this is *important*."

Panic bled from Kaylee's voice. "I don't understand how you could do this to me or to him. Tell me what's going on."

I hated that I was doing this to them. Letting them down. But what was I supposed to do? Walk out on Kas? This was my responsibility. I would make sure he was fine, that his brain was just fine behind that beautiful face of his, and then I could get the heck out of here and put this all behind me.

"I'll explain it all later. I just . . ."

Kas moaned in pain from behind the curtain.

I cringed.

Yep.

That was all on me and my dumb laser-sharp focus.

"I have to go. Just . . . please do this for me. Please, Kay-Kay?"

"Fine. But you owe me big."

Relief blew from my lungs. "I know. I know. Anything, and it's yours. Tell Daddy I love him, and I'm really sorry. I'm sure he'll be over to kick my ass in the morning."

"You know he will."

That I did.

My eyes blinked open, my senses disoriented as I tried to make sense of my surroundings. Where in the world . . .

Memories from yesterday came rushing back.

Hitting Kas.

Coming back to the hospital.

Missing the premiere.

Falling asleep on this stupid little chair with my neck kinked to the side still wearing a tight red-sequined gown. I was sure I made quite the sight.

Gathering my bearings, I stretched, stood, and peered over at Kas, who was lost to sleep, the medication they'd given him to take away his pain surely taking him there. For a moment, I let myself stare at him.

God.

He really was beautiful.

His cell phone rumbled on the table next to him, the name Dominic appearing on the screen. It stopped before it started right back up with the same number.

Hesitating, I bit my bottom lip, wondering if I'd be overstepping by answering it. But maybe he'd been totally wrong about having no one and someone was actually worried about him.

What the heck? I figured I owed this to Kas to find out.

"Hello?" I answered, keeping my voice super quiet so I wouldn't wake Kas.

"Who is this?" the voice demanded.

"Um . . . Elle?" Why that came out as a question, I didn't know, but the irritation in this guy's voice had totally set me on edge.

"Shit . . . that asshole missed his audition for pussy?" he muttered. "How he thinks he's ever going to break into the movies and then pulls stunts like this is beyond me."

I bristled, anger sliding free. "Excuse me?"

"Listen, sweetheart." He said it as if I was an ant beneath his shoe. "This is his agent, put him on the phone, pick up your panties off his floor, and get the hell out. He's late. Again."

"You're an asshole."

I ended the call, gritting my teeth, looking back at Kas, who hadn't even stirred.

Damn it.

He was an actor.

Of course, he was.

Or probably at least wanted to be since I'd never seen his face before I'd seen it on that billboard.

Old hurt wound itself around my heart.

No doubt, Kas was just like the rest of the assholes in this city, running around doing whatever they had to do to make it, hurting anyone who got in the way, climbing all over you like you were nothing but a stepping stool.

I pushed out a sigh before I turned to the television hanging from the wall, set to silence.

But there was no missing what was blipping across the screen.

My best friend Kaylee.

Sweet, innocent, Kaylee who had never had a one-night stand in her whole life.

Scaling down the wall as she sneaked out of the house of the most sought-after movie star in all of Hollywood. Wearing her gown from last night, nonetheless. The act caught on camera and smeared all over the trashy Hollywood station.

"Fucking actors," I muttered under my breath, grabbing my bag and flying out the door.

My best friend was definitely going to be needing me this morning. And Kas was just going to have to figure things out for himself. Because I sure didn't have the capacity to get any closer to a man like him.

Not with the unsettled way he made me feel.

Nope.

Not again.

four

Kassius

I see the twenty-two missed calls from Dominic, and I'm sure the number forty-seven that hovers over my text notifications are all from his as well.

"Fuck." Whatever they have dripping through my IV has taken the shooting pains away from my ankle, but my head is throbbing like a bitch.

"Mr. Cowen," the older doctor from yesterday announces as he enters my room, drawing the curtain closed behind him. I hear my roommate on the other side moaning in pain, and I momentarily feel bad for the poor sucker. At least I got the door prize of a princess with a sassy mouth and looks that all but stole my heart for my trouble.

"Doctor," I greet him, clearing my throat.

"I must say, wearing a helmet saved you from having an extended stay with us. You'd be shocked by how many more serious head injuries I see from motorcycle accidents. You're very lucky," he smirks. "CT scan was clear. No internal damage, and we'll have you follow up with your primary care doctor for the concussion. Nutrition has your breakfast outside, and once we take one last look at that ankle of yours, you're cleared to go. I'll submit discharge papers once I'm done doing my rounds."

I nod and push the button on the remote that raises the back of my bed slightly higher. I'm woozy, and I hate that feeling, but I know I needed the pain meds for my ankle last night.

With my eyes finally adjusting, I look around the room, noticing the blanket and a pillow sitting in a pile on the chair next to my bed. Did I dream that Elle was here? Those meds had me fucked up pretty good last night, and I swear she was here, looking like a dream.

A soft voice announces a, "Good morning," just as a woman in scrubs carries in a tray full of breakfast foods, scrambled eggs, sausage, fruit, oatmeal, juice, and water. My stomach rumbles as the aroma fills the air.

I devour the food in front of me and stare at the phone as more messages and calls come in . . . all from Dominic. When the phone finally stops vibrating, I lift it up, swipe the screen and tap Elle's name before the phone starts ringing.

A hesitant voice answers, "Hello?"

"Morning," my gruff voice responds.

I can hear the long sigh she releases before she says, "Hi, Kas."

"Looks like they're cutting me loose in about an hour. Gonna need a ride, Princess."

"Stop calling me that," she whispers into the phone. "Can't you take an Uber?"

"Uber? Seems like the least you could do would be to pick me up . . . considering you almost killed me."

This time she doesn't try to hide the long sigh she lets out. "Fine. I'll be there in an hour." She disconnects the call and a smile pulls at the corners of my mouth.

"Looks like this ankle will be able to be cast in about two days. Keep it elevated and iced. The swelling should continue to decrease prior to casting. We'll call in some pain meds to your pharmacy—"

"Don't." I stop the doctor right there. "Don't like the way they make me feel. I'll be fine with ice and some Tylenol." He nods in understanding as he adjusts the last Velcro band on my splint.

"Transport is here to take you downstairs. Do you have a ride coming or do we need make medical transportation arrangements?"

"Got a ride," I say, swinging my legs over the side of the bed. The medical transport employee pushes a wheelchair up, and I hobble over to it on my good leg before dropping into the seat. I see the silver BMW parked outside the large glass sliding doors, hazard lights flashing. Elle sits in the driver's seat, playing with her long hair that's been pulled up into a messy bun on top of her head. Aviator glasses hide the beautiful brown eyes that stole my heart the second I saw them.

"Right here," I tell the transport as he pushes me up to the car door. Elle doesn't bother to get out to help, she just unlocks the door and offers me a tight smile.

"Got it?" the transport asks, as I push myself up and hobble again on my good leg. "Got it." I balance with my hand on the roof of Elle's sleek car. The transport hands me a drawstring plastic bag that holds my leather jacket and the shoe I can't wear on my bad foot. "Thanks, man." I tell him and he nods as he turns away.

Once I shut my door, Elle lifts her sunglasses from her face, sticking them on top of her head. She does a quick once over, assessing me from head to toe. The late afternoon sun casts it's warm rays across her beautiful face and my heart jumps in my chest.

"Does it hurt?" she asks as she presses the triangle button that shuts off her hazard lights.

"Doesn't feel good," I respond. She cocks her head to the side and narrows her eyes at me for a moment before pulling away from the curb.

"No shit, Sherlock. I just wanted to know if the pain was unbearable. Last night—"

"You were there?"

She glances at me, and I wish she'd just focus on the road now that I know what a terrible driver she is.

"You put me down as next of kin, Kas. The hospital called to fill out paperback and guarantee funds for your CT scan."

I smirk. "You're the closest thing I have to family here, Elle. Everyone else is back in the Midwest."

"Family?" She snorts, her eyebrows jumping on her forehead.

"Someone needed to tell them what to do with my body in the event I died." I choke back a laugh.

"You're so dramatic. I barely tapped you with my car."

"You tried to run me over."

"Gahhhh!" She lets out a frustrated groan, which makes me rumble with laughter.

"I'm just busting your balls, Elle. Relax." She inhales sharply and turns to look at me.

"Where am I taking you?" she says, a little more calm than she was a second ago.

I shift in my seat to look at her more closely. Tan arms stick out from her fitted black tank top and thin, long legs poke out from her faded, ripped jean shorts. I shouldn't be the one gracing billboards, it should be her. She's a natural beauty. You can tell not a thing on her body is enhanced.

"What?" she says, taking another quick glance in my direction.

"Nothing."

"Where am I taking you, Kas?" Her voice hitches in annoyance.

"Home."

"What's the address?" she says, lifting her phone and tapping her GPS app.

"You should know, Princess. You live there." A huge smile spreads across my face just as she hits the brakes . . . hard.

Elle hasn't said a word to me since I explained that I needed her to take care of me. With my bum ankle, I needed rides to the orthopedic specialist to get a cast and, of course, will need help just managing my day-to-day tasks . . . which basically entails rest, but she doesn't need to know that.

I can see her jaw tick in annoyance, but she doesn't dump me on the curb like I expect her to. With my arm slung over her shoulder, she helps me get from the car, to the elevator, and to her front door.

There definitely isn't a grin trying to pull on my lips as she huffs and puffs and tries to catch her breath.

Nope. Nothing to see here.

I may have rested a little more of my weight on her than needed, but I really needed to play this up.

"Sit," she orders, as she pushes open her door and we step into the most insane condominium that I've ever been in.

"Holy shit, Princess," I remark as I take in the sleek kitchen, wood floors, and a view that spans the entire downtown Los Angeles skyline. I whistle loudly and run my hand across the marble countertops as I hop toward the giant leather sectional in the living room. "Someone is living large in West Hollywood."

That earns me another eye roll.

This condo is beyond amazing, how the hell she can afford it is beyond me. It's modern, chic, and a combination of wood, stone, and everything luxury.

"I need to use the restroom. When I'm done, I'll get you set up out here on the couch." She points to the long, white leather centerpiece. It's definitely the biggest couch I've ever seen . . . and looks uncomfortable as hell.

She shimmies down the hallway to what I assume is the guest bathroom. Looking over my shoulder, I can see the master bedroom, just off the living room, its double doors open wide. I push myself up and balance a hand against the wall as I hop to Elle's room.

Considerably more comfortable than the rest of the house, her king-size bed is covered in a plush white comforter and lined with probably twenty pillows of all sizes. Hobbling over, I slide onto the far side of the bed and lean back, making myself comfortable.

That red dress I thought I saw only in my dreams hangs at the end of a garment rack, and a pair of red heels sits on the floor next to it. She really did have somewhere to be last night . . . yet, she was at the hospital with me. Guilt crept in for just a moment until I heard her voice.

"Oh no. No. No. No. This is not where you're staying."

"Oh, Princess"—I smirk—"but it is. That thing you call a couch is much too hard and definitely too uncomfortable for me to stay on. I mean four to eight weeks is a long time to sleep on what looks like a slab of granite!"

If looks could kill, I'd be dead. Her shoulders rise as she takes in a deep breath.

"Kas." My name from her lips is nothing short of a growl, and it goes straight to my dick. Fuck, I love when she's feisty.

"Relax, Elle. It's going to awesome being roommates."

five

Elle

He was in my bed.

The asshole was in my bed.

He was positively infuriating.

Against my better judgment, I'd let him convince me to bring him back to my place after he'd used those damned dimples on me, telling me he needed a ride to get his cast applied on Tuesday.

I didn't even know the guy. Hell, he could be a serial killer, which I'd been quick to point out. I didn't just bring strangers to my house.

His response? To bust up laughing as he told me I was the most ridiculous woman he'd ever met.

That didn't mean I hadn't snapped a picture of him and sent an email to myself. You know, just in case I went missing and the detectives needed a pointer at who was responsible.

He'd only laughed harder and said whatever made me feel better. Once he calmed down enough to breathe, he promised he'd be on his best behavior before he'd once again reminded me that I owed him.

But this?

I pointed at him. "First of all, this is *my* room. You aren't allowed to sleep here. And four to eight weeks? Um . . . no. You can stay here until you get your cast put on, and then you're out, buddy."

A triumphant grin hit his face. "You hit me with a car."

I set my hands on my hips. "And this is the first time you've been in real danger of me killing you."

He laughed. Freaking laughed. That was right before he started peeling his shirt over his head.

"What in the ever-lovin' h—"

The words failed me.

All thought.

All rationale.

The only function I had was my mouth dropping open. That and my panties that up and went *poof.*

Apparently, I was so off-base about that whole Photoshop thing. Because the man . . .

He smirked. "Things are about to get really uncomfortable if you keep staring at me like that."

He promptly went to work on the same shredded jeans he'd been wearing yesterday.

I sputtered over the panic.

"Don't you dare," I finally managed.

"What?" he asked, away too innocently as he worked them over his hips and down his massively muscular thighs.

Of all things holy.

He was wearing those same underwear.

I had a freaking underwear model in my bed. An underwear model who smoldered and grinned and threatened to twist me up in a knot of need.

One who also wants to be an actor, that little voice warned me in my head.

He tossed his jeans to the floor and pulled back the covers, settling himself deeper into my bed. "Are you coming, or what?"

"I'm not sleeping with you."

He arched a sexy brow. "Define sleeping."

"I will stab you."

"Now who's the serial killer?"

I screeched a frustrated sound. "Kas, listen, I'm really freaking sorry I hit you with my car, but you can't sleep in my bed."

He pushed up onto an elbow, shifting to the side to stare at me from across the room, playfulness still swimming around those plump lips. "What, you afraid you can't resist me?"

"Resisting would imply you were going to try something with me."

"Put back on that dress, and I just might."

Incorrigible.

He dropped his smirk. "I'm tired, Elle, and I know you have to be, too, since you spent last night sleeping in a chair. Get in bed. I won't try anything."

My resistance fell, and his goading was back.

"You don't have to look so disappointed."

I huffed. "Not disappointed."

Nope. Not at all.

All I could hear was his chuckle as I stormed back into my en-suite bathroom and to the massive closet tucked in the back of it. I went right for the dresser in the middle and pulled out the bulkiest pair of sweatpants and baggiest T-shirt I had.

I changed quickly, muttering under my breath the whole time, trying to quiet the damned nerves buzzing through my body when I tiptoed back out into my room.

What was I doing?

So maybe I had a reputation of being a little flighty. Spoiled and pampered without a care in the world.

But that didn't mean I wasn't careful. That I didn't put thought into my life and work for the things I wanted most.

And I didn't want this.

The attraction that filled the air. The way my tummy shook when I stepped into my room and Kas shifted to look at me from where he had his head resting back on the pillow. And I sure as hell didn't want the scatter of butterflies that flapped through me when he sent me a smile.

It was a smile I hadn't seen him wear before. Something soft about it.

Tentatively, I flipped off the light and sat on the side of my bed. I gulped a big breath and slipped under my covers. Turning my back to him, I laid so close to the edge that I was pretty sure I was going to fall off.

"It's a big bed, Princess."

"Not big enough," I muttered under my breath, clinging to my covers for dear life.

"Relax," he said. There was no missing the mischief that spun out with the word.

"How am I supposed to relax when there's a stranger in my bed?"

"How do you ever get laid when you're always so uptight?"

"Uptight? I'm the furthest from uptight."

But somehow this boy had me completely spun up.

I could smell him, his warm scent that he seemed to naturally radiate, all sex and man and danger. There was something about him that promised all of those things.

"So . . ." he prodded.

"So, what?"

"How do you ever get laid?"

"Are you looking for pointers?"

He laughed. Warm and seductive. "Don't worry, Princess. I have no issues when it comes to women. I just thought you might need a little help."

"Nope, I'm all good."

"I bet you are."

Damn him. How did he do that? Push me and pull me and tempt me?

Silence gathered around us, somehow dense and palpable, as if I could feel each twitch of his packed, hard muscle. Every tiny movement. Every pulse of blood that ran through his veins.

"Thank you," he finally murmured from behind me.

Something foreign bottled in my chest, and I clutched my blanket tighter. "For what?"

"For taking care of me. Not a whole lot of people in this city would do that."

That feeling tightened. "You're welcome," I whispered so quietly I wasn't sure he heard.

"Don't feel bad, Princess, I think I might just enjoy this ride."

six

Kassius

The slightest hints of coconut pull me from my sleep. It's then I realize my face is nuzzled into the crook of Elle's neck, my arm snaked around her waist, holding her tight against my chest, and my leg squeezed through both of hers.

I am spooning Elle.

Tightly.

And I fucking love it.

My lips brush against the back of her neck as I readjust my head, and I pray to God she doesn't feel the massive hard-on that's trying to break free from my briefs. She stirs for a second, but the steady sound of her breaths tell me she's still sound asleep.

I could hold her like this all day.

Every day.

What the hell has gotten into me?

Just then, she twists in my arms, falling to her back. My hand rests on top of her bare stomach where the giant tee she went to bed in rode up sometime in the night. My fingers barely brush the soft, tan skin just above the waistband of those also too big sweat pants.

Even in her ripped Guns-N-Roses tee and gray sweatpants

covered in paint, she's fucking sexy as hell. Maybe even more so than in that stunning red dress she was wearing the other night. I reach down and readjust my boner, praying to God that the little fucker doesn't get me in trouble . . . he usually does.

I hold Elle for another half hour before she finally opens her eyes, staring at our entanglement, only she doesn't push me away.

"Hey," I mumble, my face so close to her neck she has to turn her head to make eye contact with me.

"Hey," she answers quietly.

"I guess sometime in the night we ended up like this—"

She swallows hard, the muscles in her neck contracting as she barely nods.

"It's nice." Nice. That's what I say . . . *nice*. Ugh. I'm an idiot. It's better than nice. It's fucking perfect. She feels perfect.

"Mm-hmm," she says before pulling her shirt down, her hand brushing mine away as she does so. After untangling her legs from mine, she pushes herself up. "I'm going to make breakfast." She sits on the edge of the bed, dropping her head forward. It looks like she's trying to catch her breath, and I can't help but smile.

Then she's up and moving toward the door, stopping and turning back to me just before she gets there. "Feel free to clean up. There are clean towels on the rack in the bathroom."

I nod, and her eyes hold mine for a moment longer than they should before she turns and walks out of the room.

Stepping into the utterly giant shower, I'm in awe of its size. There are showerheads everywhere, and there isn't a square inch of the shower where you aren't under a stream. I try to put a little weight on my ankle and end up yelping in pain. Hopping carefully under the water I steady myself against the shower wall.

Pulling the bottle of shampoo from the built-in shelf, I squirt a good amount into my hand. It smells just like Elle. Coconut and sun, and I want to lather my entire body in her scent. Massaging my scalp with both hands, the warm water rinses the silky shampoo from my hair. Just as the suds travel down my body, I feel myself losing balance. With my eyes closed, I reach for the wall just as my feet slide out from underneath me.

"Shit!" I yell on the way down, taking every bottle Elle has on her shower shelf down with me. The sounds of every bottle hitting the tiled floor is amplified in the glass-encased shower, and I cringe when my bare ass hits the floor.

"What is happening?" Elle screams as she comes bursting through the door. Rubbing the soap from my eyes, Elle's face suddenly appears. Her eyes wide, her lips forming the perfect O as she stares at my naked self lying on her shower floor.

"You gonna stare at me or help me up, Princess?" I ask, snapping her out of her trance.

"Are you okay?" She pulls her eyes away from me, a blush creeping over her cheeks and down her neck.

"Fine, but a little help would be nice."

She closes her eyes and takes a deep breath as she opens the shower door slowly and steps inside just enough to help me.

She isn't beyond the water's reach, though, and it hits the side of her face as she leans down a bit to get the leverage she needs to pull. Her tee is soaked and sticks to her every curve. Her nipples hard, little buds underneath that thin black material.

"Good?" she asks, her voice cracking when she gets me up.

"Never been better."

She releases my hand and quickly turns around as I grab her forearm stopping her. "Need your help, Elle. I can't do this and balance myself on the slippery tile."

Her brown eyes look into mine, and I can see the conflict on her face. I can see how I affect her. She gives her head a little shake but doesn't say no. I reach for the sponge, which somehow managed to stay on the shelf and she bends to retrieve her body wash off the floor.

She squirts a healthy amount of it into the sponge and cautiously reaches out, placing the purple sponge on my shoulder. Her eyes never leave mine as something unspoken passes between us. Maybe it's gratitude, maybe it's lust, but right now, her hands moving that sponge in a circular motion across my chest is the best fucking thing I've ever felt.

"Turn around," she whispers, and I place both hands on the wall. One of her hands presses against my back as the other starts at my shoulder with the sponge again. Her motion is slow and gentle and goddamn if my traitorous dick doesn't betray me again. She stops at my lower back before starting again with the back of my thighs.

"Missed a spot there, Princess," I say when I look over my shoulder at her.

"You can wash your own ass," she scoffs, shoving the sponge at me. I turn around and her eyes go where I hoped they would.

Down.

Down.

Down.

I wanted her to see what her touch does to me . . . and does she ever. Her mouth hangs open and she inhales sharply before looking back up to me. She is standing in the shower, soaking wet, the sweat pants so heavy from water they're sliding off her hips.

"Like what you see?"

She snaps her mouth closed and scoots back, looking up at me.

"No need to get your feathers in a ruffle. I'm just messing with you, Princess."

Even though I am fully capable of washing myself, I really am grateful for her help, although my intentions to get her in the shower with me may have been slightly selfish.

I want to peel those clothes off her and press her against the tile wall—instead I meet her eyes again and mumble, "Thanks for the help."

She nods nervously before turning around and fleeing, leaving me needing, wanting more of her.

Her touch.

Her body.

Just her.

I hobble aimlessly out of the bedroom and find Elle standing at the large kitchen island, now dressed in a pair of skintight yoga pants and tank top. Her long, wet hair hangs in strands, and she looks at me nervously, a blush crawling across her cheeks before she offers me a shy smile.

"We'll have breakfast on the patio." She motions toward the wall of glass that opens to a large balcony while she's chopping fruit on a cutting board. I manage to hobble—a little more dramatically than I had been—through the living room and outside before dropping onto a comfortable chair.

The view of the Hollywood hills is simply amazing. Elle joins me, carrying a tray. On it sits a bowl of scrambled eggs, fresh cut fruit, yogurt, granola, and two mugs full of steaming hot coffee. I inhale sharply as the aroma of the coffee hits my nose.

"Hope you like healthy." She sets the tray down before taking the seat across the table from me. She reaches for a mug of coffee and leans back into her seat. "Help yourself, I'm sure you're starving," she urges when I don't immediately make a move for the food.

Pulling the mug of coffee from the tray first, I sip the hot liquid carefully. It's like a drug in my veins, and I smack my lips after that first sip. She watches me carefully, her eyes narrowed.

I try to break the tension that I undoubtedly caused by having her help me in the shower. "So maybe we should start over, huh, Elle?"

"Start over?"

"Yeah, like, let's pretend you didn't try to kill me by running me over . . ." She rolls her eyes and sets her mug of coffee down. "If we had just run into each other, let's say"—I tap my chin—"at the market." I grin widely at her. "I'd walk over to you and have some really cheesy line about how beautiful your eyes are." I pause and really look at her. "And you'd smile and fall for my pick-up line. Then we'd end up at some café having coffee, much like we are now. We'd have to do all the getting-to-know-you questions like normal people that date do."

Her eyebrows shoot halfway up her forehead when I say that. "We aren't dating, Kas."

"Yet," I amend and continue. "So, Elle, what is your last name?"

She plucks a strawberry from the fruit bowl before popping it in her mouth. She chews, swallows, then answers my question.

"Ward."

"Elle Ward." I smile at how her name rolls off my tongue.

"Nice to meet you, Elle." A smile tugs at her lips, but she doesn't respond. "What do you do for work?"

She runs her finger around the rim of her coffee mug and looks away from me, out over the L.A. skyline that seems endless.

"Advertising," she says quietly. She seems distracted, distant, and suddenly somber.

"It's your turn to ask me two questions." I pick up the bowl of scrambled eggs and dump most of them onto my plate. She shakes her head and raises the mug of coffee to her lips. "Come on, Princess. How else are we going to get to know each other?" I joke with her.

She continues to shake her head slowly before she finally settles her eyes on mine.

"Tell me one more thing about you then." I prod her for more information. I'm not sure if the look on her face is annoyance, frustration, or disdain, but she watches me carefully before setting her mug back on the table. This time instead of a soft click of porcelain against glass, it makes a loud *thud*, as if the sound in and of itself is trying to convey whatever her expression can't, and she leans in, ever so slightly.

"One more thing, huh?" she asks, licking her bottom lip. "This is probably the most important thing you'll need to know about me, Kas."

I'm intrigued. Hell, I'm almost fucking giddy she's going to share something with me. I set my fork down and wait for her to share.

"Spill it, sweetheart," I coax her.

She takes a deep breath before releasing it slowly. She studies my face, her eyes dropping from my eyes to my lips and back up. "I don't date actors."

The words are firm, decisive, and forceful. Those four little words squeeze at my heart, and I swallow hard against my suddenly dry throat.

Without another word, Elle stands from the table, taking her mug of coffee, and walks back into her condo. I hear her mumble something about, "Fucking Hollywood," just before a door slams in the distance.

seven

Elle

It'd been a long day by the time I climbed into the elevator from the garage floor. So it kind of sucked that I felt almost reluctant to press the button for the penthouse floor.

I mean, it was my home. I should have absolutely no reservations with walking through its doors, and I wouldn't if I hadn't have been so crazy and left a model / up-and-coming actor to his own devices for the entire day.

How stupid.

But I just couldn't be in that space anymore after waking up wrapped in his arms this morning and then finding him completely naked in the shower, having to get into it with him, of all things, the man flaunting himself like he was some kind of model.

Oh right.

He was.

That, I could handle.

Kind of.

Because it'd left me flushed and heated. It'd left me wanting the man in a way I most certainly couldn't allow myself to pursue.

So I told him straight.

I don't date actors.

I didn't.

Not after Christopher. I'd learned that lesson the hard way.

The very hard way.

I beat back the unsettled feeling and jabbed at the button, my stomach lifted to my throat as the elevator quickly ascended. It wasn't as if I was some timid virgin, but still my knees were shaking when the metal doors slid open.

Blowing out a breath, I headed down the hall and slid my key into the lock, turned the knob, and prepared myself for whatever I might find inside.

What I did, I was most definitely not prepared for.

Kas was in my kitchen.

Shirtless.

Attraction beat through my body, heavy and hot, and the most delicious aroma glided through the air and struck my senses.

I was pretty sure I was standing there with my mouth hanging open when Kas shot me a grin from over his muscled shoulder.

Good God, the man's back was a work of art. No filter needed. He was the real deal.

Hell, he might as well have been on one of the huge canvases decorating my designer living room, signed and stamped.

A priceless original.

"Welcome home, Princess."

"What are you doing?" I asked, somehow taken aback and surprised and totally caught off guard.

Here I'd figured the guy had probably trashed the place. I'd definitely been planning on using that as an excuse for kicking him the curb.

I didn't know if I felt defeated or relieved.

"Uh . . . what does it look like I'm doing? Making you dinner."

"Your ankle is broken," I argued, thinking if he could make us a gourmet dinner, he could most definitely take care of himself.

Because the man needed to go.

He was way too gorgeous and apparently a little too sweet. You know, all mixed up with that infuriating personality of his. Or maybe I was really just furious at myself. Because there I stood with my mouth dry and my girly bits on high alert.

Bad girl.

He stirred the sauce he had simmering on the stove. "That it is . . . and it's honestly throbbing like a bitch from standing here for the last hour, so why don't you get that gorgeous ass in here and fix us some plates? Not sure I can stay standing for a second more."

Every word that fell from his full lips was delivered with a straight shot of sexiness and the faintest hint of a tease.

Swallowing all the confusion swirling through my mind, I slid my laptop case onto the floor and headed his direction. "When's the last time you had any pain medication?"

He glanced at the clock on the microwave. "Sixteen hours ago?"

"What on earth? Are you insane? The doctor instructed you to take it every four to six hours."

He grimaced a little as he tried to balance on his good foot. "This is Hollywood, baby, but the last thing I'm looking to do is become another sad cliché."

Crack. Crack. Crack.

There he went, hammering into my reservations.

"It's prescribed, Kas."

"It always starts out that way, doesn't it?"

I gulped. "I guess a lot of times it does."

"So, it's just better not to go there," he said before he let his sexy mouth tip up at the side. "Besides, I figured you could kiss it, make it all better."

"Not on your life."

"Hey, you almost took my life."

"The dramatics."

His smile widened. "I came here with the dream of becoming an actor, remember? I just can't help myself."

That was what I was afraid of.

Moving the rest of the way into the kitchen, I shooed him away, hating that I didn't mind it all that much when he used me for support as he hobbled over to the bar. I plated our food, sat beside him, and answered a few of those questions I'd shot down this morning.

Where did I go to school and why did I choose advertising and did I ever want to do anything else.

ULCA.

I love being behind the scenes.

Never.

On the last question, I left out the part where I'd once dreamed of being a director like my dad. He didn't need to know was who my dad was. I'd already slipped up this morning when I'd given him my last name.

Luckily, he hadn't caught on, the name too mundane and common to spark any sort of recognition.

"That was delicious," I told him when we finished, gathering our plates.

He quirked a brow. "A compliment, huh?"

My head shook. "Just the truth."

He sat back in the stool with a satisfied sigh, patting his flat, defined belly.

Was it wrong I wanted to lean down and lick it?

"Good enough to keep me around? A man could get used to this."

I shot him a wry grin. "What, making me dinner?"

"Nah, seeing your face when you walk through the door after a long day at work."

I ignored him and his damned infectious charisma and charm. Ignored the way my entire home felt different when I moved to the sink to quickly do the dishes. The way his presence filled the massive, vacant space, making it feel warm and comfortable.

I rinsed our plates and leaned over to place them in the dishwasher. I gasped when I suddenly felt him behind me.

The front of his jeans pressed right into my behind. My thoughts were instantly back to this morning, the way he'd taunted me with that huge cock.

The boy didn't fight fair.

He leaned over me, his lips brushing my cheek as he reached around and dropped the silverware into the basket. "You didn't think I was going to let you do dishes all by yourself, did you?"

Nope, not fair at all.

Before I gave into the want speeding through my veins and pressed back, I whipped around, almost losing my footing when he was right there, his hands going to the outside of my arms to steady me.

Funny how he only had the use of one foot and I was the one close to dropping to my knees.

What the hell was wrong me? This was L.A., for God's sake. I was no stranger to a pretty face.

But there was something about him that felt . . . different.

Or maybe it was just my issue that I'd always loved to ride on the wild side.

He reached up and brushed his knuckles down the side of my cheek. I shuddered through a breath, my stomach tightening in a knot of want. "I meant it," he murmured softly, his dark eyes moving across my face.

"What?" It came out a little hard because I couldn't let this boy get to me.

"I think I could look at your face every single day and never get tired of it."

My chest tightened, and I forced out a scoff. "You're delusional. You've known me for all of a day."

"Call me a good judge of character."

He leaned in and my heart spun and my lips parted.

Oh God. He was going to kiss me. He was going to kiss me and that made me nothing but a damned fool.

I jerked back, almost sending him toppling, trying to smooth myself out with my shaking hands. "I think we'd better call it a night."

He grimaced before nearly sending me reeling from the power of his smirk. "Trying to get me into bed already, huh, Princess?"

I rolled my eyes and headed for my room. "Not on your life."

His laughter bellowed against my walls that no longer felt so big. "You sure don't mind betting on my life, do you. Careful now. You never know what kind of trouble you're going to get me into."

He truly was delusional.

Because the only one in trouble was me.

eight
Kassius

This time, I am legitimately hobbling. Hobbling because my ankle fucking hurts like hell. A combination of throbbing and burning, but the pain was worth it.

The look on Elle's face when she walked through the door after work and saw me cooking was priceless. A look of confusion, gratitude, and downright appreciation all twisted into one on that beautiful face of hers.

"Wait! Let me help you." Elle rushes over to meet me at the edge of bed, helping me get situated and propping my foot onto extra pillows. I sigh, loudly, in relief when my back hits the mattress and my foot finally rests at a comfortable incline.

My phone is plugged in and sitting on the nightstand, and Elle flicks the television on, tossing the remote onto the bed next to me. "Need anything else before I go clean up?" She pulls a large silver bracelet from her wrist and works the backs off her earrings before tossing them onto her nightstand.

"Nah, I'm good."

She nods, turning to walk toward the bathroom where her walk-in closet is attached. I noticed it yesterday. It's more than a closet, it's a fucking spare bedroom, with a large island in the middle and more racks and shelves than I could ever fill. Her closet is as big as my bedroom at my apartment, and there isn't a square inch that isn't covered in Elle's clothes, shoes, and purses.

Just as I settle in and begin to relax, my phone buzzes. I chance a glance and see Dominic's name flashing across the screen . . . again.

I can't avoid him forever, but goddamn, it's been nice not to be rushing out the door the last few days to work out at the gym or run to auditions and photo shoots. I almost forgot what it felt like to relax . . . and it has felt nice. I mute the television as I grab my phone.

"Dom," I say, answering his call. He wastes no time getting right to the point.

"About goddamn time you answer the phone. I've been trying to get ahold of you." He sounds out of breath, as if he's calling me while he's out for an evening run.

"Yeah, sorry about that. I've been resting, staying off my ankle." It's amazing how easy the lie rolls off my tongue. I hate lying. It isn't in me, but I have been avoiding his calls for no reason other than wanting to spend my time with Elle.

He barks at me. "Well, answer the phone when I call."

"Sorry, man." I rake my hand over my face and apologize. Dominic is a pushy motherfucker, but rightfully so. This last year has been a whirlwind of modeling contracts and supporting roles in feature films as we wait for the big one to land in my lap, all thanks to him.

He has connections and is one of the best agents in Hollywood, and he has yet to steer me wrong. The last thing I want to do is model, but he promises it will open doors for me.

And let me tell you, the second I hit magazine spreads and billboards in a pair of designer underwear, everything was suddenly on the table for me. Modeling, movies, television . . . all were mine for the picking. The guy knows what he's doing.

"A script landed on my desk today, it's perfect for you."

"Tell me more," I grumble and turn to see Elle brushing her teeth in the en-suite bathroom, her long, dark hair piled on top of her head and her perfectly round ass squeezed into a pair of tight pajama shorts that leave little to the imagination.

"It's a Roger Ward film, Kas. You'd be perfect. This role was meant for you."

Roger fucking Ward. Hollywood's hottest director right now. This man can make or break careers. Dominic definitely has my attention.

I sit up a little straighter in bed. "Send me the script."

"Where to?" he asks, his voice piqued with interest. "I stopped by your apartment twice today, but you didn't answer."

Because I conned my way into staying with the most beautiful woman I've ever met.

She frustrates me, excites me, and fucking turns me on. She also tried to kill me with her car, I want to tell him, but I refrain.

"Ah, yeah. I'm staying with a friend. She's helping take care of me since I can't really get around right now."

"She?" he questions, and I can hear the challenge in his voice when I mention my friend is a female. I've told Dom for months that my sole focus is my career, that I have no desire to date, and that women are nothing but trouble.

I told myself I wouldn't let a woman get in the way and derail my dreams, and I was adamant about that, until Elle. She's a force I hadn't been expecting.

"She," I respond, "has been helpful in my recovery. The sooner I heal, the sooner I can get back to the grind." I look across the room again and back to Elle, who's standing at the bathroom counter rubbing lotion all over her perfect face. My stomach twists into a giant knot when I think about leaving here . . . not seeing Elle every morning and every night, not curling up to her in this bed, my nose pressed to her neck.

"What's the address, Kas? I'll have it delivered to you first thing in the morning. This is it, this is the one." His voice hitches with excitement. "You need to do whatever it takes to get you back to one hundred percent . . . and fast."

The bathroom light flicks off, and Elle saunters across the plush carpet toward the bed, looking like a vision. Her natural beauty on full display.

"You got it," I say, lowering my voice. "I'll text you the address.

You know, I'm willing to do whatever it takes to make it, Dom. That's why I'm here, this is my dream." As Elle approaches the bed, she cocks her head to the side, her eyes narrowing ever so slightly though the rest of her face is expressionless.

What is she thinking?

Dominic's voice pulls my thoughts away from Elle and back to our conversation.

"That's what I like to hear. Don't let your ankle or any other distractions get to you. This role is butter in your hands. It's yours to lose." He actually lets out a sly laugh just as I disconnect the call.

nine

Elle

It hits me then. Really hits me.

The hottest man I'd ever seen was in my bed, and he was actually kind of a nice guy, sweet and charming and thoughtful and oh so wrong for me.

It was never more obvious than when I realized he was on the phone talking with his agent.

This boy was an actor.

And actors? They acted, and the only thing I could do as I stood there was wonder if all that sweet, caring charm was just a part of the scene. The scene where the good-looking man manipulated the stupid, foolish girl.

I didn't want to be her.

Not ever again.

He placed his phone back on my nightstand and turned a soft smile in my direction. "What are you doing over there looking so serious?"

I released a nervous giggle and fiddled with the hem of my tank.

"Makin' ya nervous, Princess?"

I rolled my eyes at him. "I'm not exactly the nervous type."

"Is that so? You're looking awful nervous to me. I won't bite."

"That was exactly what I was wondering."

His brow lifted in question.

"Whether you bite or not," I filled in his unspoken question.

His laughter was a rumble. "You're worried about me biting?" He swept a hand over his leg that was propped on the pillows at the base of my bed. "I'm kind of invalid right now. I think it's you I should be worried about."

Another eyeroll. "Hardly. I couldn't hurt you if I tried."

"Funny, since you're the one who put me in this state."

He grinned a grin that tightened my belly into a knot of lust. I came to the quick conclusion that kind of charm couldn't be feigned. He'd been born with it.

"Are you ever going to let me live that down?"

"I don't know," he drew out the tease.

God. This boy made me forget myself. Lose my head. Forget the very promise I'd made myself. Because I was moving that way a bit, loving the way he was looking at me.

"What do I have to do to make it all go away?" So what if I injected a little pout into it, hips swaying just a fraction as I moved across the floor.

His gaze swept me. Head to toe. "You can start by getting that cute little butt in this bed. Maybe then we can talk about it."

I planted my hands on the bed. "It's that all it is going to take?"

He shifted so he was propped up on one elbow so he was facing me. His abdomen flexed, muscles hard and defined. The very distraction that had gotten me here in the first place.

"How about we start there?"

He reached out and grabbed me by the wrist, hauling me onto the bed. I yelped and then laughed as I hit the mattress. Instantly, his fingers went to my ribs.

Oh my God! Was he actually tickling me?

I howled with laughter, gripping at his hands, trying to pry them away. "Oh my God, Kas. Stop. Stop. I'm going to pee."

It only encouraged him, and his hands were moving all over, jabbing across my belly, grabbing on to my inner thighs, but then he was over me, tapping his fingers right into my thundering chest.

He slowed, the energy he'd whipped into the air stilling around us, hugging us tight.

Awareness taking hold.

He stared down at me while I stared up at him.

Enraptured.

So close to falling.

My tongue darted out to wet my lips.

He groaned. "I wouldn't do that if I were you."

"Why's that?" I said, so throaty I was pretty sure it might have been a plea. An invitation for him to come closer while the rational side of me was imploring him to stop. To get the few things he had there and get out. Go home.

He'd managed to plant both hands on either side of my head, his body twisted off to the side as he hovered over me to keep his foot guarded.

"Because if you do, I'm going to kiss you."

He held his weight, pushing up so he could let his eyes trail over my body.

Lust shimmered. A glimmer from his smooth, olive skin.

Would one kiss be all that bad? A mistake? It wasn't as if I didn't know how to handle a man.

Gazing up at him, I wondered if I could really handle *this one*.

He was every single thing I'd promised myself I'd never go for.

The epitome of what I was guarding myself against.

When he looked back, a smirk had taken to his face. "And if I kiss you, you'll be begging me not to stop."

There it was.

The evidence that I really couldn't handle this man.

I wiggled out from beneath him, searching around in my brain for the same kind of commitment I'd had when I'd party until six in the morning back at UCLA and still dragged my ass out of bed in time for my eight o'clock class.

It was brutal and hard, but I did it because I knew that, in the end, it was going to pay off.

Kas huffed a little sound, his expression telling me he had no idea how to read me when he plopped back onto his side facing me.

He hesitated for a second before he said, "I meant what I said this morning."

"I did, too," I told him, a bit of regret making its way into my words. "I told you I don't date actors."

He pursed his full lips, as if he'd immediately put a lid on all the flirty teasing. "And why's that, Elle? Seems to me it narrows down your options, considering you live in Hollywood."

"Actors are assholes."

He laughed.

Actually laughed.

He rolled onto his back and weaved his fingers through his soft hair.

Something shivered through me.

The urge to do it for him.

Damn, had he slipped right under my skin.

I mean, God, he'd basically shacked up with me, and I didn't know a single important thing about him.

All except for the one that mattered most.

He rolled his head toward me, brown eyes narrowed. "I have to admit, I've met a few assholes out there, but it's a pretty bold assumption for you to make about *every* actor."

"Is it?"

"Hello." He waved his hand dramatically in the air. "Hugh Jackman. Tom Hanks. Nicest guys in the world. Tell me you wouldn't date Hugh Jackman." He grinned when he said the last.

I giggled, rolled to my side. I couldn't help but be drawn to his outlook. The way he was so easy-going. Maybe this city hadn't had the time to go to his pretty head.

I rolled onto my side so we were facing each other, both my hands pressed under my cheek as my gaze wandered over his face.

"Where are you from?"

"Chicago," he said, still smiling.

"And what brought you here?"

He hooked his thumb over his shoulder toward the windows overlooking the city. "That Hollywood sign you have such a great view of? Could see it all the way from Illinois."

He let his gaze glide to the ceiling. I could almost see him picturing the sign as a child.

"Really?" I chewed at my bottom lip, looking at his profile.

"Really." He nodded before he shifted his face back in my direction. "You know, through the television."

Laughing, I reached out and smacked his chest. "You jerk."

He grabbed at my hand before I could pull it away, pressing it flat across his chiseled, strong chest.

Nope, he did not fight fair. Not at all.

"No, but seriously, all I ever talked about growing up was moving here one day." His voice turned wistful. "The day I turned eighteen, I packed a bag, hopped into my car, and drove straight through until the sign came into view."

Maybe he was different, after all.

He shifted to look back at me. "What about you?"

"I've lived here my whole life."

"Ah, so you've probably run into your fair share of actors."

Regret and the last vestiges of hurt that reminded me to never make the same mistake again pulled tight against my ribs.

"You could say that."

He stared, waiting, still holding my hand over the pound, pound, pound of his heart.

"I dated one once," I quietly admitted.

"He was no Hugh Jackman?"

A bluff of laughter filtered out. "No, he was no Hugh Jackman. He was just using me until he didn't need me anymore."

Blindfolding me with his beauty and charisma and promises, using me as a step stool. One to get to my daddy.

It'd hurt in the worst way when I'd found out.

"You want me to kick his ass?" He grinned. So sweet.

Beauty. Charisma. Promises.

What if Kas was the same?

"Stop that," he chided.

I frowned, and he reached out and smoothed the pad of his thumb between my eyes. "Stop thinking I'm just like him. I promise that I'm not," he answered for me.

"But what if you are?" Like a fool, I asked, the question nothing but an admission of vulnerability.

"And what if I'm not?"

"I'm not sure I know how to tell the difference."

He blew out a resigned breath before something carefree took to his expression. "Come here, let me cuddle that cute butt of yours."

"We are not cuddling." Of course, it was nothing but laughter echoing from my walls when he wrapped me in those ridiculously strong arms and tugged me against his chest.

He smacked my bottom.

I yelped again.

"Oh, Princess. There's so much more to you than another pretty face."

I buried my face in his neck, my arms bent and pressed between us, as if I were subconsciously putting a barrier between him and my heart.

Because I was starting to wonder if there wasn't so much more to him, too.

ten

Kassius

Elle and I have fallen into a sort of routine. She goes to work, and I stay at her place, reviewing scripts that Dom sends me and making sure dinner is ready and waiting when she gets home each night.

Yesterday, she fulfilled her end of the deal and took me to get my cast. Since the swelling started to subside, it doesn't hurt so damn much, which makes it easier to get around. Only I'm not ready to let Elle know that.

I still have her help me shower, tuck me in every night, and she makes us breakfast every morning before she leaves for work. While she's gone, I do my best to get some sits up in, plank work done, and I think I did eight-thousand arm curls with Elle's tiny ten-pound dumbbells I found tucked away in her closet. I was so fucking bored yesterday, I popped in one of her yoga DVDs and did yoga for an hour. Shit's hard, who knew?

Guilt kicks me in the stomach every night when she walks in the door, looking tired. The last thing she needs is to be taking care of my ass, but here I am. I'm not ready to let her go yet.

I've basically become a goddamn domestic goddess, ordering groceries online and planning menus. I was prepared to clean, too, until the cleaning lady showed up and scared the living shit out of me. Elle forgot to tell me she had someone come every other week to clean her condo, do her laundry, and change her sheets. The older lady was just as surprised to see me propped on Elle's couch in my underwear as I was to see her bounding through the door with an armful of cleaning supplies.

Once the awkwardness of our introduction wore off, we laughed about it, and Camila was all too kind to do my laundry as she was doing Elle's. Her interrogation told me she was genuinely invested in Elle, and I appreciated that about her. It was also nice to have some company during the day, and she let me practice my shitty Spanish with her while she laughed her ass off at my pronunciation of basic words like *pollo*, or chicken. Who knew it wasn't pronounced *po-lo*?

Camila helped me prep the marinade for the chicken I was going to grill tonight and she chopped vegetables, too. She kept shooing me away and telling me to, "Sit, *Mijo*. You're hurt," and pointing at my ankle. I was hoping to pick up some additional pointers from her, but she insisted on making me prop up my foot while she finished prepping our dinner. I gave her some extra cash, as I know meal prep is outside the duties Elle hired her for.

Knowing that my days are numbered before Elle catches on to my bullshit, I decide to make tonight count. I pull out the big guns—candles, placemats, wine . . . the whole nine-yards. The chicken that marinated all day is grilled to utter perfection, and the veggies are seasoned and roasted perfectly. I even have a goddamn cheesecake delivered from that high-end grocery store down the road.

I open a chilled bottle of pinot grigio and pour a glass of beer into a frosty mug for me. Never been a big wine drinker.

Elle stumbles in the door around seven thirty, just like she does every night, dropping her purse on the floor next to the door. She kicks off her heels, which she doesn't need because she's already long and lean.

Her eyes dance around the kitchen, and I swear I see a flash of disappointment before she finds me sitting at the table in the dining room that most likely never gets used.

"Kas?" I have the lights off, and the candles add just the right amount of light to the dining room. Enough to see everything but dim enough to make it perfectly romantic.

I tap the glass top dining table next to her place setting as she saunters over. "This is amazing," she remarks, taking it all in. The candles, flickering brightly. The glass of wine that sits poured and waiting for her, the food all plated and ready to be eaten. All for her. Because she deserves it, and the look on her face makes me happier than I've felt in . . . dare I say, ever?

"I'm glad you like it." God, I'm an idiot. I make it sound like I ordered her a fucking pizza. "I mean, I wanted to do something special for you, Elle. You've been really helpful . . ." I pause, lost for what I want to say next. In caring for me? By letting me stay here?

"I did run you over," she cuts in with a hearty laugh. She slides into the seat next to me and reaches for the glass of wine. "I mean, the least I could do is help you, right?" Her lips pull into a tight smile.

I nod and take a sip of my beer.

She waves her free hand across the table. "You really did all of this?"

"Well, I did have a little help from Camila," I tell her and her eyes grow wide, and she slaps a hand over her mouth.

"Oh my God, I forgot about Camila!" She gasps and chokes on her wine.

"Well, she walked in and I was sitting on the couch in my underwear." I gesture over my shoulder with my thumb toward the living room where that god-awful couch sits.

"No!" she says loudly, stifling a laugh.

"Yes!"

"I'm so sorry." She finally laughs. That beautiful face of hers tipped back and a smile so wide it pulls at the corners of her eyes. She's simply stunning.

"Eat." I point to her plate. "Before it gets cold."

She proudly tells me all about her day and the new account that her team just landed and I can't help but smile as I listen to her. She finally pushes her plate away, when she can't take another bite, rubbing her stomach in discomfort.

"That was amazing. Seriously. I haven't had chicken that was that delicious in a long time."

"I'm glad you enjoyed it." I pull her almost empty wine glass from her hand and refill it. "It's the least I can do." I catch her looking at me. Her face somber, her eyes a little glassy. "What?"

She shakes her head a little as I hand her back her drink. "Nothing."

"Tell me."

She takes a sip. "Really, it's nothing." We look at each other for a long time. Something unspoken passes between us before I finally push my chair back.

"Come on." I reach for her hand. "Let's go out on the patio."

She takes my hand and stands, her other hand gripping her wine glass tightly. When I should have dropped her hand once she was standing, I decide not to. Instead, I lace my fingers through hers, giving her soft fingers a little squeeze, guiding her to the patio.

"This view," I say as we sidle up to the glass railing of the patio, "is unbelievable."

She nods and points to the lit-up downtown Los Angeles skyline. "This view is what sold me on the condo," she says. "I wasn't sure I wanted to live in West Hollywood, but this"—she stares out over the sky—"makes it worth it."

Our elbows brush against each other, and the breeze gently lifts her long hair, whipping it around her face. Instinctively, I reach out, tucking a long strand behind her ear. Elle's casual stance stiffens when my fingers brush against her cheek as I capture another loose strand of hair, tucking that one away, too.

Heart racing.

Blood swooshing.

My hand falls from her cheek to her shoulder, and my fingers follow a trail down the soft flesh of her arm to finally come to a rest on top of her hand. Her fingers widen, inviting me to lace mine through hers, my palm on top of her hand.

Elle angles her body toward me. Her eyes heavy, her long lashes fluttering with each slow blink of her beautiful brown eyes.

"What are we doing, Kassius?" she asks, her voice shaky and barely above a whisper. I shrug, not sure I'm ready to tell her exactly what I'd like from her.

"We're two people getting to know each other." I use my free hand to pull her closer. Her pink lips are parted, and she pulls her bottom lip between her teeth, worrying at it gently. "I've enjoyed getting to know you, Elle. I want to know more about you." I brush the front of my fingers over her cheek, and her head tilts to follow the gesture. Her eyes flutter closed as I brush her cheekbone up to her temple and back down.

Maybe I'm a coward for doing it this way, but I don't ask, I just take.

Leaning in, I press a soft kiss to her supple lips. Lips that taste like wine and sugar. So goddamn sweet. I can feel her inhale sharply, yet she doesn't pull away from me. Taking that as my cue to continue, I kiss her again. Perfect, sweet kisses. Over and over. This time, she returns them.

She reaches for my face, her hands trembling on my cheeks as she deepens her kiss. It's both the sexiest and most intimate kiss of my life. That muscle in my chest kicks up a notch, and I can feel it beating wildly against my ribs.

Pulling her lips from mine, she inhales loudly and takes a step back. We both pant heavily as we regain our breath. Her eyes fall from mine to her feet, which she shifts back and forth nervously.

"We shouldn't do this." Her words are quiet but stop me dead. My gut twists as I take in the conflict on her face.

"We'll take it slow." I reach for her hand, but she pulls it away, not allowing me to touch her. She takes another step back, putting more distance between us while shaking her head from side to side.

"Give it a chance, Elle." My voice tinged with what almost sounds like desperation.

I'm fucking begging her to give us a chance. I've known this beautiful stranger for a week, and I can't imagine my life without her.

She closes her eyes and takes a shaky breath. "I don't think this is a good idea."

ONE **WILD** RIDE

My heart sinks as the weight of her words sink in, but I won't let her have the final say in this. She doesn't get to dismiss us so quickly. "Well, I do. So, roll with it, Princess."

I take a demanding step forward and press a quick kiss to her forehead before hobbling inside the condo and heading toward the bedroom. Goddamn if I'm going to let that beautiful girl dismiss what we both just felt.

It is more than lust.

It is more than intense.

It is everything.

eleven

Elle

What had I just done?

Oh, that was right, I'd let Kassius kiss me.

The sexiest man alive.

The untouchable, gorgeous creature set on display on billboards, who had a body like a chiseled sculpture.

The dangerous, aspiring actor, no doubt trained to be just like every other limelight-hungry, vain, shady, selfish prick willing to do whatever it took to make it to the top. Either pushing someone else down and climbing right over the top of them to get to those heights, or, more than likely, sleeping their way there.

The sweet boy who'd spent the last week living in my apartment? That was the one who got to me the most. The one who had me questioning every promise I'd ever made to myself. Prodding at me to just give it a try.

Hell, I should give it up and have a little fun.

But, somehow, I knew Kas wouldn't leave me unscathed, and a little bit of fun would turn into a whole ton of heartache. That, and when he looked at me tonight and told me he wanted to get to know me better, it really meant he wanted to get inside every inch of me.

Body and soul and mind.

Those penetrating eyes saw way deeper than just the surface.

I paced my bathroom, wrung my fingers, blew out a strained breath.

If he was looking at me so deeply, then why was I so scared to give him chance? If he was only looking for a stepping stone, why would he need to get to know me?

To earn your trust, you dimwit, my mind screamed at me, while my heart was screaming its own defense, hating that I'd let Christopher scar me so badly that I was terrified to let anyone else get close to me.

Because having a little fun was one thing?

Letting this man in was an entirely different story.

I knew doing so would be giving up on every resolution I'd made, all those staunch declarations belittled by the need this boy had lit inside me.

Banging shook the bathroom door. "Elle," he called from the other side, the sound of his voice so close he had to have his face pressed right up to the wood.

"What do you want?" It flew out with more spite that it deserved, but Kassius Cowen had me on edge.

"You," he returned.

Damn him.

"Oh, yeah? Well you can't have me." It was all a petulant defense when I turned toward the door and crossed my arms over my chest.

A warm chuckle filtered through the door. "Is that so?"

"Incredibly so."

"How about you stop hiding in your bathroom and we talk about that?"

"There's nothing to talk about."

"I beg to differ."

I didn't say anything.

Another pound, though this one softer, I figured with the back of his fist. "Come on, Elle. Open the door. You've been in there for over an hour. I have to pee."

"Use the powder room off the living room."

"My leg is hurting."

Worry and twinge of guilt twisted my stomach. Dang him. I edged forward and slowly clicked the lock.

The second I did, the door banged open, and Kas was sauntering in. My gaze raked him, the man wearing nothing but a pair of shorts hanging way too low on his waist, all those muscles rippling with every step he took.

"It doesn't look like your leg is hurting to me," I managed, flustered, heat gliding through my body.

I couldn't help it. As soon as I saw him, I was struck with the way his lips had felt pressed against mine. It'd been a startling kiss in its softness.

Something so different from what I'd imagined in all those moments when I'd let myself imagine *too much*.

Oh, but I knew right then that, if Kas got his hands on me again, his kiss would be different.

"You're right. Leg doesn't hurt."

"You lied?" I screeched.

His dimple made an appearance, that little spot alone a tool that wiped out a whole layer of my walls.

What was wrong with me?

He stalked closer, and I was backing up when his low voice hit the air. "Call it a fib. I just needed to check on you."

My butt hit the counter, and I gasped. "Oh."

He came even closer, his nose almost brushing mine. "See . . . you've been talking nonsense, so I figured I needed to check to make sure your thoughts were working themselves out."

My eyebrows flew up so fast it kind of made my head spin. "Me? You think it's me who isn't thinking right?"

He brushed his knuckles up my cheek.

My lips parted, and my knees went weak.

"Definitely," he said. "You said something about me kissing you being a bad idea."

"It is a bad idea," I returned. "And it doesn't have anything to do with my thoughts being out of order. The only bad idea I've had was bringing you here in the first place."

There was no fire behind it.

No firm belief.

Because I wanted him there. Had been anxious every single day when I left work to get home, knowing he'd be in my kitchen, making me dinner, which was all kinds of an awesome bonus.

The real prize was getting the view of seeing this man standing in my kitchen.

Stealing my breath every single day.

Like he was doing right then.

Though this time, he was sucking them down, inhaling me as I was inhaling him, something fierce moving around us as he stood there wearing a satisfied smile on his face as he watched me.

"And you said I'm the liar?" He whispered it at my jaw. "Besides, you bringing me here was my idea. You agreeing to it was the beginning of the best decision you ever made."

He peppered those words along the length of my jaw until he was murmuring them in my ear, the vibration of them tumbling through my body.

He set his hand on my opposite cheek and plucked a kiss at the very edge of my lips.

Shivers cascaded down my spine.

"Kas."

He slipped his hands to either side of my neck, his lips moving against mine. "Shh . . . don't think. Just feel it."

That was the problem. I could feel him everywhere.

My body pitched.

He grinned. I could feel it. Right against my lips.

"You really wanna feel it, huh?" he teased.

"Kas." I wanted it to come out as hard, but it fumbled out on laughter.

Really, I should put this gorgeous man in his place because I was pretty sure he was a master at getting whatever he wanted, especially in a town like this.

I squeezed my eyes closed against the thought.

We all had our dreams.

Was it wrong for me to judge him for his?

But him having those dreams wasn't really the problem. It was just I wasn't sure how I could ever fit into them. Even if he wasn't an asshole, his drive for fame would always come first.

As if he could sense my worry, he slid his palms over my shoulders, all the way down my arms, until he was twining his fingers with mine. He stepped back, staring at me. "Hey . . . I mean it, Elle. I like you a lot, and I want to see where this goes. Even if it takes us some time to get there. For you to trust me."

Disbelief filled my smile. "I don't know what to make of you."

He widened his eyes playfully. "That's why you're supposed to get to know me."

"And what if I don't like you?" I ribbed, biting my lip and loving the feeling that filled my chest.

Because I felt it chip away. A hardened piece of anger that had closed me off from a lot of relationships.

Hurt that was heavy.

Right then, I felt lighter than I had in a long time.

He dropped one of my hands and began to walk backward out of the bathroom so he could still watch me as he pulled me along with him.

Was it wrong he was still the hottest thing I'd ever seen in that cast? Hell, the boy could sell a broken ankle as the next best thing.

A single brow arched, his sexy mouth twisting in a smile. "Not like me? Come on, Elle, don't tell me that mind isn't working right again. No chance you aren't gonna like me." He pulled me to his chest, his mouth back at my ear. "In *every* way."

Shocked, I gasped, hands on his bare chest, before he was chuckling and leading me to my bed that he somehow owned.

How the hell was I supposed to sleep with him after I'd tasted him?

All my lady bits fangirled.

They totally loved the idea.

I sucked in a breath and climbed onto the bed behind him. He was still on his knees when I laid down on my pillow.

He planted his hands on either side of my head and dipped down closer, a sexy kind of arrogance leaving him on the words. "It's going to happen, Princess. Count on it."

twelve

Kassius

Her mouth opens but then snaps shut quickly.

Elle's heart beats so wildly I can damn near feel it as I watch the throbbing pulse in her neck. My gaze falls from the curve of her neck to the soft, supple flesh of her breasts that are peeking out of the sides of her tank top. Slivers of perfect C cups taunt me, teasing me to reach out and touch them.

"Kas," she breathes, her voice husky. I divert my eyes back to her face just as my dick begins to harden. *Damn it.*

"Elle." I mimic her tone and cock my head to the side. Her brown eyes holding mine, I look for a sign that she wants me, that she wants more. Her pink, pursed lips are an invitation that I gladly accept. I want them all over my body. Perfect, plump, and soft.

Leaning in, I press a soft kiss to the corner of her mouth and feel her chest deflate before she inhales sharply when I deepen the kiss. As I lower myself on top of her, her thighs spread, making a home for me between her legs. A place I've dreamed of being. Thin sleep shorts do little to hide the heat I feel coming from her center.

I will have her. Every square inch of her will be mine. Just not tonight. Elle needs to understand I want more than just a romp in the sheets with her. I want it all. I want to own her heart, body, and soul, and I'll wait for her, but damn it, I *will* have her.

My nose grazes her jawline before finding that sweet spot right behind her ear where I press my lips. She mewls and tosses her head from side to side as I nip at her ear lobe.

"Bad idea," Elle mumbles as her hands grip at my bare sides, her fingers gently pinching the flesh just above my hips.

"Perfect idea, Princess."

Instinctively, I rock my hips into her center, letting her feel me through the thin fabric that separates us. I feel her physically shudder when my boxer-covered dick brushes against her warm opening.

This woman.

How the hell did we get from her damn near running me over to right here?

To her bed.

To her winding a place into my heart. In one week.

"Oh my God," she mutters as I rock against her core again, her hips bucking back against mine, a natural response.

"That's right, baby. You'll be praying to every spiritual figure you can name and everyone in between when I finally take you." My dick probes at her, and it takes every ounce of my self-control to back off.

"Mmmm," she barely manages to get out before she arches her back, pressing her chest into mine. My hand snakes up underneath the hem of that too little tank top that leaves nothing to the imagination.

She's all soft flesh and everything beautiful all in one perfect package. Her sun-kissed skin pebbles with goose bumps at my touch.

My large hand glides up her side, stopping at the bottom of her rib cage. Brushing my thumb against the soft curve on the underside of her breast, she arches her back tighter into me. An unspoken request to touch her.

I could plunge into her right now and lose myself, but I won't. Tonight, I'll take only a small piece of her.

Pushing her tank top up and over her chest, her heavy breasts fall from where they were held by that flimsy material, and I inhale sharply. Her pink nipples, all puckered into hard little buds are begging for my mouth. Her chest rises and falls with each shallow breath she takes.

Her eyes flicker from mine to her chest before her fingers dig into my sides, pulling me closer to her.

"Bad idea," she mumbles again. Who she's mumbling too, I don't know. Surely not to me, because every kiss, every brush of my finger sends her body into overdrive. Definitely not a bad idea.

"Best." I press a kiss to her neck. "Idea." I press another kiss to the space between her breasts. "Ever." I finally pull one of her nipples into my mouth, giving it a firm suck.

"Shiiiiit!" She yelps, her hands moving from my sides to my back. Her fingernails press into the firm muscles that line each side of my spine.

"You like that, huh, baby?" I chuckle, moving to her other breast, running my tongue in soft circles around the other nipple. Her legs fall open wider in response.

Her breathing has turned to panting, and I'm so fucking turned on that if I don't stop right now, I'll blow my load right here. Reaching down, I adjust my erection as I slide off Elle, pausing our fun for tonight. I prop myself up on my side and readjust her tank top, pulling it back into place.

She stares at the ceiling, her eyes blinking slowly as she regains control of her breathing. Her head rolls to the side, and her eyes meet mine. Something between lust, sadness, confusion, and utter joy swirl around in her expression.

I reach out and lace my fingers through hers, placing our linked hands on top of her chest before leaning in and pressing a sweet kiss to her lips. "Good night, Elle."

"Night, Kas," she says quietly, squeezing my hand. I pull her closer to me and cradle her against my chest as I close my eyes and fall asleep with her in my arms.

thirteen

Elle

"Oh my God, you're back!" I said to Kaylee into my cell. Okay, I squealed it. I couldn't help it, not when my best friend had galivanted off to London with one of the biggest superstars of our time.

Paxton Myles.

She was so in for an interrogation. The last time I'd seen her, she'd been crying her eyes out in her living room while she watched the paparazzi talk about her life like it was an HBO show. The next thing I'd known, I'd seen her face flashed on the screen that she'd run off to London with Paxton.

Totally out of the blue.

Totally in the limelight.

Every kind of speculation cast their way.

It was just reason number two thousand eighty-two a smart girl shouldn't pick her dates from the Hollywood pool.

Worse was I'd tried to call her umpteen times, and every single one of my calls had gone to voice mail. To say I was concerned was an understatement. Especially when I was the one who'd put her directly in the path of that speeding train.

Begging her to attend my father's premiere and then missing it in favor of running over the sexiest man alive.

Gah.

My life.

"Tell me you're alive and in one piece and I don't have to race over to kick Paxton Myles's ass."

She giggled.

My reserved best friend, whose only desire in life was to be a kindergarten teacher, giggled.

"Paxton is harmless," she said, a sigh sliding into the words.

Oh God. She really was in deep.

"Paxton Myles? Harmless? The world's most eligible bachelor? Womanizer extraordinaire? We are talking about the same person?" My voice had gone incredulous.

"No longer eligible," she corrected, her breath hitching as she whispered it like a secret into her phone.

"You're really serious?"

"Really, really serious."

"What in the world has gotten into my best friend?"

"Paxton Myles." She couldn't hold back her laughter. She busted up in it, and there was nothing I could have done but laugh along with her.

"So, the rumors are all true. You really have become a Paxton Myles Slut."

"Um . . . no. Paxton Myles became my man. Big difference. Big, big difference."

Holy crap.

She *was* serious.

My brows narrowed. "Where are you staying?"

Her tone dropped again, as if she were trying to keep her confession to herself. "At Paxton's."

"It sounds like we need a couple of bottles of wine to catch up over."

"Definitely. So much has changed. And speaking of that, with all the stuff that happened so quickly in my life, you never fessed up to what happened the night of the premiere."

"It's way less interesting than what happened to you at the premiere."

"Liar." It was all a tease.

I sighed.

Kaylee sobered. "Hey. What's wrong?"

Nerves tumbled through me. This stuff was so much more Kaylee's territory. I was supposed to be a fortress. No one even coming close to getting into my heart. And there I was, anxiety clawing through my senses and need pulsing through my body, stirring everything up so I didn't know up from down.

The worst part was the growing affection that thought it would be a good idea to build itself up right in the middle of me.

"It's nothing," I told her.

"I call bullshit," she returned.

Another sigh, and I rubbed my temples as I came to a stop at the light.

"So, I kind of ran someone over the night of the premiere."

"What?" she screamed.

Crap.

Sometimes my delivery was totally bad.

"He isn't dead or anything," I said.

"Oh, well that's good to know." Pure sarcasm. She sucked in a couple of breaths, calming herself. "So, what's the long face for? Is he trying to sue you or something?"

"You can't even see me."

"I can totally see you. Right now, you basically look like someone kicked your puppy."

Automatically, my attention darted to the rearview mirror.

Yep.

Kicked puppy.

That was exactly what I looked like.

"No, he isn't trying to sue me."

"Then what?"

"He wants to go out with me. Date me." The last came out as if they were dirty words.

"And what's wrong with that?"

I hesitated for a second, trying to gather my thoughts and my emotions that didn't know what direction to go. "He wants to be an actor. He's a fame chaser."

Silence hovered on the other end of the line. Kaylee knew all about Christopher. What I'd gone through. The way he'd used me because of my family name and then tossed me aside when he no longer needed it anymore.

"And what makes you think he's anything like that jerk?"

"Aren't they all the same?" Bitterness bled out with the words.

She inhaled, and I could almost see her softly shaking her head. "No, Elle. I used to think so, but I learned firsthand not to make assumptions about people based on what they look like to the rest of the world. Had I let that guide me? I would be missing out on the love of my life."

Tears pricked at my eyes.

Damn it.

This was so not me. I didn't have emotional reactions like this.

But Kas had me so spun up. Tied in knots. Wanting things I knew better than to want with a guy like him. I should know better than allowing Kaylee's words to soothe me.

I *knew* better.

I had the mashed-up heart to prove it, and I didn't think I could survive that kind of betrayal again.

"Maybe you got lucky," I murmured quietly.

"Maybe you'll get lucky, too. Just because he wants to be an actor doesn't make him a jerk, Elle. Christopher was an asshole. A straight asshole who used you. You can't just assume this guy wants the same thing."

"He doesn't know who I am." I rushed, desperate to admit it to someone. Relief followed, as if I'd purged a lie that had been crushing my chest. "He doesn't know," I whispered a little quieter.

"And why is that?"

I pushed out a sigh. "I don't know . . . because I wanted to protect myself, I guess."

"Or maybe you wanted to see if you should give him the chance," she returned.

One of those tears slipped free. "Kay-Kay."

She laughed lightly. "Don't pretend like I don't know you. I totally know you. You like him."

"That's the problem. I like him too much."

"Then see how it goes."

"And what if it goes badly?"

"Then *you* tried. *You* gave it a shot. *You* trusted and opened up your heart. Because living afraid isn't the right way to live. You know that, Elle, no matter how carefree you spend your days and your nights, there will always be something missing if you don't open yourself up to possibilities. If this guy doesn't see that and doesn't appreciate you for who you are and not who your family is, then he's the idiot. He will be the one missing out."

She lowered her voice. "Just don't let your fear make you miss out. You deserve to be happy, Elle. Truly happy. Give yourself a chance."

That would mean giving Kas a chance.

My trust.

Was I ready for that?

I was excited when I stepped onto the elevator that led me to the top of floor of my building.

Kaylee was right.

I needed to give this a chance. Set my fears and hurt and reservations aside and see where this went. Kas didn't know who my father was. He wasn't using me. We could just . . . *be* for a while. Know each other outside of our connections and goals.

Outside of the fame.

My smile was wide when I swung open the front door.

And like Kas had been so many times before, he was in my kitchen, preparing dinner again. Though, tonight the small table in the nook was set, candles dancing, Kas dressed in fitted dress pants and a button-up that made him look so damned good my knees knocked.

He spun around when he heard me enter, excitement on his face. "It's about time you got home. I've been waiting for you."

A low chuckle climbed my throat as I dumped my things inside the door. "Um . . . I get home at the same time every day. Did you expect me earlier?"

"A man can hope, can't he?"

"I think you do just fine around here while I'm gone."

"Not even. It's lonely as fuck. I'm about to go out of my mind around here during the day."

"Then maybe it's time you went back to work and stopped milking that broken ankle for all it's worth," I teased.

His teeth raked his bottom lip.

Damn, that was sexy, and my mind raced back to last night when it'd been my lip he'd been nipping at.

"That's actually what I wanted to talk to you about."

I snapped back to the present when I realized he'd phrased his words as a question. "What's that?"

He rounded the corner and came toward me, his limp improved but noticeable. "Sit with me."

He took my hand and led me to the table, pulling a chair out for me. "Such a gentleman." I tried to make it light, but there was a tremble in my voice. What was he up to?

He sat opposite of me and poured me a glass of wine. "What's going on?" I asked, suspicion in my tone.

He fiddled with his mug, glancing between me and the growing foam. "These last couple weeks have been the best I've had since I got to Los Angeles."

Emotion pitched through my chest. Squeezing my heart. Could I believe that? That he was really wanting this as much as I was wanting him?

The problem was, that terrified me.

I swallowed around all the questions and pinned on a playful smile. "I guess it hasn't been so terrible with you hanging around."

"I'm serious, Elle. Since I met you . . ."

He looked away for a beat before he looked back at me. "I want to share stuff with you, and I've never wanted that with anyone else before."

"You do?"

Another wall crumbled.

Crashed to the ground.

"Hell, yes." He reached over and grabbed my hand from over the table, a rush of excitement rising to his face.

"Come with me to the Golden Globes next Sunday night. I know it's short notice, but my agent called and said he has big news to deliver. The second he told me, I knew I wanted you to be the one on my arm when I receive it. You're that girl, Elle. The one I want at my side when I walk the red carpet. The one I want to come home to at the end of the day. The one I wake to in the morning."

Expectancy filled his grin.

As if he thought I was going to hop up and congratulate him.

Throw my arms around his neck, kiss him wildly, and tell him I wanted all of those same things.

Instead, panic froze my tongue, and every promise I'd ever made myself rose to the surface. The one time I'd gone with Christopher to an awards show was the same night he'd told me that he'd finally made it big and having a girlfriend would only hold him back.

He'd given me the whole it's not you it's me line.

Of course, that had been after he'd signed on my daddy's line—a big fat contract that had made him a star.

I suddenly couldn't breathe. I clutched the edge of the table, wheezing for the nonexistent air.

Panic filled Kas's face. "Elle, what's wrong?"

I squeezed my eyes closed, trying to pull myself together. But it was no use. "I need you to leave."

Kas rocked back. "Are you kidding me right now?"

"No." I had to force it between clenched teeth.

He shook his head in disbelief, roughing a hand over the cropped hair on his head. "I just poured my heart out to you and invited you into the most important part of my life, and you tell me to leave?"

It was the first time I'd heard Kas truly upset.

No jest in his voice.

No witty comeback that tripped me up in laughter.

"I'm sorry," I told him.

He scrambled to take hold of my hand. "Come on, Elle. I don't know what's going on with you, but I want you there. I want you there with me. It won't be the same without you."

"You don't even know me."

Air huffed from his nose, and he withdrew his hand when I didn't take it. He rocked back in his chair. "Yeah, you've mentioned that. That's because you refuse to let me in."

"I told you, I don't date actors."

He shook his head. "That's what this is about? The fact I want to be an actor? Nice."

"Just go home, Kas." The words were propelled by fear. The only defense I had.

I needed him to go.

Leave before I fully gave in.

I was the fool who had thought I could keep those worlds separate, and here they were, already colliding.

Anger rolling from him, he pushed to standing. My nerves rattled at my insides when he leaned over and pressed his hands to the table, his face butted up to mine as he cocked his head. "Tell me one thing, Elle? Is that the same bullshit excuse you give every guy or do you just not like me?"

I blinked at him. Trying to find stable ground. To hold on to the reason I had to do this. "You're the one who pushed for this."

He inched closer, his mouth brushing mine, my breath hitching in my throat. "Because I felt something. Every fucking time I looked at you, I felt something. And I thought maybe—just maybe—you felt something, too."

When I didn't say anything, his mouth twisted in disappointment, hurt blistering from him like rage. "Then I guess I'll get out of your way."

He pushed from the table and hobbled away, his leg seeming to drag behind him as he went.

I heard him banging around in my bedroom.

Five minutes later, he appeared in the doorway, slinging his huge duffle bag over his shoulder and resignation on his chiseled face. He moved toward the door, dragging his foot behind him as he struggled to carry the bag.

I should have gone to him. Stopped him or helped or did *something*.

But I didn't know how to change our circumstances.

Who we were or who either of us wanted to be.

Because Roger Ward's daughter couldn't show up on the arm of another up-and-coming actor.

Not again.

But when he paused to look back at me when he pulled open the door, none of what passed between us felt like acting.

Hurt.

Longing.

Regret.

And when he stepped out and slammed the door shut behind him, I was sure he walked out with a piece of me that I wasn't ever going to get back.

fourteen

Kassius

"Kas! Over here!" The loud—and familiar—tabloid reporter's voice catches my attention. As I turn my head, lights begin to flash wildly. I paint on a crooked smile that sends the press into a bigger frenzy. More lights, more flashes, more shouting.

"Kas!"

"Kas! Look this way."

"Over here!"

Dom stands next to me with his cell phone pressed to his ear, most likely dealing with another needy client. He nods at me to start the red carpet walk without him, he'll meet me inside the theater. Press lines aren't his thing; after all, he's just an agent. Hell, he didn't even want to come with me tonight, but the bastard felt bad for me after Elle declined.

I don't even know what the hell happened with Elle. One minute, I was asking her to join me, and the next, she was yelling at me to go home.

"Kas! Is it true you landed the campaign for Calvin Klein?" I just smile politely and don't answer. That deal is freshly penned; the ink hasn't even dried. I signed the contracts in the limo on the way here . . . for ad campaigns for underwear *and* fragrance.

Dom pitched the deal to the Calvin Klein reps months ago, and I spoke at great length with them, only not to hear anything for weeks afterward. We assumed they weren't interested or found another fresh face, however, we usually hear *something*.

Dom shocked the shit out of me when he slapped a contract in my lap right after I slid into the limo. He said legal looked it over, and it was a solid contract, that I'd be stupid not to sign it, and then handed me a pen. He informed me that this was the first time anyone has landed both campaigns simultaneously, and they were paying me handsomely for it. To the tune of two million dollars. I damn near felt nauseous as I was signing the papers.

That kind of money is life changing. The jobs I've been taking have paid ten thousand here, fifteen thousand there, and after Dom's cut and taxes, I make out okay, but I still live in a shitty apartment and eat dry chicken and steamed veggies out of a microwave for dinner.

"Kas, what happened to your foot?" Another photographer asks as I move slowly, favoring my ankle.

Hobbling down the red carpet a little farther another reporter tosses a question at me. "Any chance we'll see you on the big screen, Kas? You've got what Hollywood is looking for." She damn near drools on herself, her smile is so big I wonder if her cheeks hurt. She winks at me as she runs her tongue over her bottom lip. Tacky.

"One can hope," I answer and turn my attention toward the line if front of me. The assistant to Hollywood reporter Brian Everfest is waving me down. He hosts the most popular entertainment program on television and radio. I slowly make my way to them, stopping along the way for a few more photos.

"Kas Cowen," Brian says enthusiastically, shoving a microphone closer to my face. "Nice to see you, man!"

"Thank you. Nice to see you, too."

"Rumor has it that you've inked a multimillion-dollar ad campaign with Calvin Klein, what can you tell us about that?"

Nothing. I think to myself. The damn contract is in the pocket of Dom's tuxedo. It hasn't even been returned to Calvin Klein yet. Besides, I want to be the one to tell Elle the news, not for her to hear about it on some sleazy entertainment show. And, for the love of God, I literally signed the damn contract twenty minutes ago in the back of that limo, how the hell do these people hear about these things this quickly?

I smile and look Brian right in the eyes, this way they think you aren't lying. "I think that's a great rumor, and I'd be absolutely honored to work for the Calvin Klein brand, but no. There is nothing official to announce." Brian clenches his teeth and tilts his head. This asshole thought he was going to break the news. Not tonight, Brian.

Changing the subject, he looks to my foot. "Can you tell us what happened to your foot?"

"It's actually my ankle." The cameraman tilts the large shoulder camera to show my tuxedo clad legs and my ankle that's stuffed in a cast. "I had a little mishap on my motorcycle and broke my ankle a couple of weeks ago. It's healing nicely, still a little sore, but nothing would stop me from attending the Golden Globes."

"Hey, man. Thanks for stopping and hope your ankle heals quickly." With a quick handshake, I move away and skip the last reporter. The press here is relentless, and I'm not in the mood for it tonight.

I amble my way through the crowds and find Dom, who's talking to some up-and-coming Hollywood producer. I smile politely, but it does little to hide my shitty mood, and he shoots me a look to settle down. As excited as I should be, I just wanted Elle to share this evening with me. She should be with me, and now I just want this night to be over.

Three after parties later, my mood has turned somber, I'm feeling the whiskey in my blood, and my ankle hurts like a motherfucker. I did as Dom asked—I showed up, made the rounds, smiled for the cameras, and rubbed elbows and shook hands with the people that counted . . . and somehow, I still feel unfulfilled. My mind, but mostly my heart, isn't into tonight because it is with Elle.

The look on her face when I asked—no, damn near begged her to come with me, was something between defeat and hurt, and I don't know why. Her walls went up, and I didn't have time to break them down before she'd demanded I leave. Her telling me to go home had crushed me. It felt like her shutting me out . . . it felt final.

The limo finally pulls up, and I slide into the soft leather bench seat in the back.

I tell the driver to take me to my apartment when the only place I want to go is to Elle's condo.

"*Go home.*" Those words Elle spoke shake me and echo in my ears while simultaneously making my heart ache.

I rake my hand over my face and pinch my eyes closed, letting the alcohol running through my veins relax my muscles. Whiskey should have helped ease my mind, let me forget about Elle, it only made it worse. I saw her in every woman there tonight.

The drive is quiet, but it still takes longer than I'd like it to. I just want to sink into my bed and let my mind rest.

We roll up to the simple, gray stucco apartment building—the place I've called home for the last two years, and the driver parks near the base of the stairs. It's definitely not West Hollywood, that's for damn sure. The driver opens the door, and I step out carefully, my ankle throbbing in my cast. Thanking him, I shrug out of my tuxedo jacket, flinging it over my shoulder as I make my way up the concrete stairs to my second-floor apartment.

The overhead light flickers as I try to get the keys out of my pocket. For the last two nights, I've stayed here alone.

I'd only been at Elle's for just under two weeks, but that doesn't change the fact that my heart hurts that I won't be curled around her soft body tonight. She's been a source of comfort, a place of peace, someone I've grown to love in a very short time.

Love.

As I hobble closer to the end of the hall, I see someone outside my door. In the dim light, it's hard to make out exactly who it is, but as I draw nearer, I know I would recognize her anywhere. *Elle.*

She sitting on the ground, her back pressed to my door. Her long arms wrapped around her knees, which are pulled tightly against her chest. Her forehead rests on those knees, and her long hair hangs around her, hiding her beautiful face.

When she hears me, she raises her head, lifting her chin to look up at me. Those beautiful eyes are swollen and red, a sign she's been crying—but she's here. *For me.* And fuck if that doesn't mean the world to me. She came here looking for *me.*

Without a word, I reach out my hand to help her up. She slides her hand into my hold and I pull gently, lifting her to her feet. Her eyes search mine. For what? I don't know. An apology? Acceptance? Now isn't the time to talk, so I open my arms, and she does exactly what I hope she will. She falls into them. Her face presses to my chest and her arms wrap tightly around me, and I hold her back.

Tighter than I've ever held anyone before because I'm not letting her go—*ever.*

fifteen

Elle

"I missed you," I mumbled at the collar of his tuxedo shirt as I clung to him, praying this was real. I pressed my nose up under his chin, inhaling him.

The sexiest man in the world.

If I hadn't known it before, I'd known it when he'd stood in front of me wearing a tuxedo, the jacket slung over his shoulder and the top buttons of his shirt undone as if he were a modern-day James Dean.

Trouble.

So much trouble.

And I was running for it.

"You're here," he rumbled at the top of my head.

"I couldn't stay away," I whispered as my hands curled tighter into his shirt.

"Good," he muttered, his warm body nudging my back against the door. I hit it with an *oomph*. "Because I fucking missed you, too."

I looked up to search his face. "I'm scared."

He reached out and brushed his thumb across the dampness of my cheek. "What are you scared of?"

"You."

He grinned a cocky grin, though his eyes were tender. "I thought that was supposed to be the other way around. You were the one who ran me over."

"Then why am I the one who feels broken?"

"I don't know, Elle, but I think it's about time you let me in on that."

"Just tell me you want me for me."

He nudged closer, his chest against mine, his breath filtering down all around.

Whiskey and warmth.

My insides trembled.

Want rising high.

He nuzzled his nose up the side of my jaw, before he whispered in my ear, "I've wanted you since the second I opened my eyes and thought I was looking up at an angel. You stole my breath then but it's my heart you're stealing now."

"Kas."

He didn't answer.

He dipped down and kissed me. Firm presses of his lips and soft sweeps of his tongue. I felt him grow hard against my belly, and a shudder ridged through my body. He fumbled behind him to get the key into the lock, and the door banged open to a darkened apartment that was probably smaller than my whole room.

And I knew it wasn't fair that I'd judged him.

He might have wanted to be an actor, but that didn't mean he didn't want me.

Backing me through the darkness, I knocked into the back of his couch, his chuckle deep when he dipped me over it for a beat and kissed me. The second he did, something fired, a fierce intensity that lit between us.

He yanked me up, his kiss becoming possessive. Demanding. "I want you, Elle. Fuck, I want you. This last week was brutal, thinking I wasn't ever going to see you again."

"I couldn't sleep. Couldn't stop thinking about you. Wondering about you. I watched you on the red carpet. You owned every inch of it, Kas. You were the most striking man there."

I could feel his grin against my mouth as he edged me into the single bedroom at the back of the apartment. "So, you're telling me that you like me?"

Gulping down my reservations, I pulled back, staring at him through the shadows. That same fire smoldered from his face as he stared back at me. The sexiest man alive, and there he stood, ready to adore me. "I think I'm falling for you."

"Good thing, baby, because I'm already right there ready to catch you."

He nudged me back, sending me tumbling onto his full bed with the blankets and sheets twisted.

My giggle bounced off the walls. "Oh, you're just going to toss me over the side."

He smirked as he worked through the rest of his buttons and then twisted out of his shirt.

My mouth went dry as he pulled the white undershirt off, and I pressed my knees together as I took him in.

Chiseled chest and golden skin and perfect, angled jaw. Standing there looking every bit the star I knew he was going to be.

He tugged at the button on his pants. "Sometimes people need a little push."

This boy had pushed every single one of my buttons.

He leaned over and worked free the Velcro straps of his walking boot and then kicked out of his pants.

My breath left me on a needy sigh.

There he stood in the exact same kind of underwear as he'd worn on that billboard that had changed everything.

Set us on this course.

It could have been nothing more than a detour, but somehow, I knew I was getting ready to embark on one wild ride.

He climbed onto the bed, crawling over me, kissing me sweetly as he pressed his hands under my shirt. His palms hot and sure against my bare skin.

Inciting a fire.

I arched.

"Impatient," he murmured through a chuckle.

"I need you."

"Think I already made it plenty clear you have me."

I stared up at him through the yellowed glow of the streetlamps filtering in front outside. "Then take me."

Then Kas.

He did.

He undressed me slowly. Differently from how he'd ever been before. And when he nestled his bare body between my thighs, he was looking into my eyes.

Pressing into my body, my mouth dropping open and my nails sinking into his shoulders as he seated himself deep.

Owning me in a way I hadn't allowed anyone to in a long time.

Wholly.

And in that moment, I gave him all my trust.

sixteen

Kassius

Around the time the sun was just beginning to rise Elle fell asleep in my arms, fully sated after we made love for hours.

Hours.

Sex has always been a means to an end for me. Get in, get off, get out. With Elle, I couldn't get enough of her. I'm afraid I never will.

I took my time exploring every soft curve, every peak and every valley on her body, and I memorized the sound of her voice, the smell of her musk, and the tremble of her body as she came underneath me countless times.

Every moan and every gasp and every tremble was a road map that I buried in the back of my head. Her pleasure was all that mattered.

Finally coming down from the high of having Elle back and our first night officially together, I closed my eyes to the soft purr of her breathing and finally succumbed to everything that'd happened in the last forty-eight hours. I thought I had lost Elle, I gained a major ad campaign, I met some of Hollywood's elite, and I got Elle back. It was one hell of a couple of days—days I will never forget

We still have a lot to talk about and to work through, but here . . . in this bed with the woman I've fallen for wrapped around me, I'm content to not speak at all. Honest to God, this feeling is the only thing that really matters. Everything else can wait.

Before I even open my eyes, I can feel her looking at me. Her long legs are intertwined between mine, and her chest pressed against mine. "What time is it?" I mumble against my dry throat as I fight to crack open an eye. The seemingly bright afternoon sun assaults me through the open curtains.

"Don't know. Don't care," she says, pressing a soft kiss to the small of my throat. "I called in sick to work." I instantly grow hard as her fingers trail soft circles down my side moving to my hip. We fell asleep naked, the sheet and comforter pooled at the end of the bed, our naked bodies wrapped tightly around each other. She giggles knowing what her touch does to me as she reaches down and wraps her palm around my hard shaft. Elle strokes me slowly a couple of times as I capture her soft lips in mine and nibble on her bottom lip.

"Don't you want breakfast first? Or lunch, or . . . Elle!" I hiss as she rolls me onto my back and suddenly straddles me with her long legs. She presses her wet core against my dick and it takes every ounce of self-control not to raise my hips and press myself into her bare. The feel of her wet opening against me is utter torture as she glides back and forth, covering me in her wetness. She narrows her eyes and rubs the crown of my dick through her slick lips, stopping just shy of allowing me inside her. My heart stammers in my chest as she reaches for the pack of condoms that sit on my nightstand and rips a foil packet open between her teeth before rolling it on my throbbing erection.

Then her mouth finds the soft skin of my neck, where she nips gently before sitting back and slowly lowering herself onto me. My fingers grip the sides of her hips, and she takes every inch of length as if she were meant for me. Only me. She lets out a loud gasp as I fill her to the hilt, her clit pressed against my pubic bone. There is a moment where neither of us moves, as we drown in the feeling, but then she offers me a devious smile. Elle uses her fingers on my chest to balance herself as she begins to ride me. Starting out slowly, she increases her pace until she's found her rhythm.

Beautiful Elle, her head full of long hair falls back over her shoulders as she rides my dick, and with every thrust, she grinds herself against me. I raise my hips to meet her descent as we find a perfect cadence with our lovemaking.

"That's it, baby," I moan as her perfectly round tits bounce each time she slides up and down on me. With every plunge, she rolls her hips and presses her clit against my pubic bone, bringing herself closer to orgasm.

I hold her waist guiding her up and down as her head falls back one last time and her body tightens around me as she lets out a guttural moan. I've never seen anything as beautiful as Elle when she falls apart on top of me. It takes me seconds to meet her climax, emptying myself into her.

Catching my breath, I run a knuckle over her soft cheek. "I'll never get enough of you, Elle."

"Mmmm," she responds as her body shudders one last time as she's still coming down. She bites her lip and closes her hooded eyes as she falls forward onto my chest and into my waiting arms. This is it. This is love. This is exactly what love feels like and goddamn if it isn't the best feeling in the world.

"I mean it, Elle. You're it for me."

I don't wake up again until around three in the afternoon. Carefully, I manage to slide out from under Elle, who is still soundly asleep, and sneak in a quick shower. She's still out when I emerge, her long hair is spilled across my pillow and her hands are tucked under her cheek. I've never seen a more beautiful woman sleep.

I chill a bottle of wine I've had for months, and order Chinese takeout for us before settling on the large sectional couch and propping my ankle on the coffee table. I open my phone to thousands of Twitter notifications, Facebook tags, Instagram posts, and endless text messages about the Calvin Klein campaign.

I guess the cat is out of the bag. I should be fully focused on the breaking news, but it's the woman who appears in the doorway with a long white sheet wrapped around her perfect body that has my full attention.

"Hey," she says, her voice raspy in that throaty, sexy kind of way.

"Hey, sleepyhead," I answer her and pat the empty seat cushion next to me, inviting her over. She holds the sheet tightly against her chest as her bare feet pad across the carpeted floor. She sinks onto the couch next to me and rests her head on my shoulder as if she's done this a million times.

"Whatcha doin'?" She asks, glancing at my phone, which lights up with more incoming notifications.

"Just checking my phone." I set it on the large square ottoman nestled into the crook of the sectional sofa. I want to tell her the news before she sees or hears it anywhere else, but right now, I just want to focus on her. "You know, it's almost four in the afternoon."

"We had a late night and an early morning." She grins up at me, blinking her tired, brown eyes. Those eyes hold love and fear and a look of trepidation as we dive into this relationship full speed ahead.

"That we did." I wrap an arm around her shoulders and hold her closer to me. "I ordered us some dinner, Chinese takeout, and I have a bottle of wine chilling. I hope that's okay."

"Sounds perfect." She hums before stretching her legs along the couch cushions next to her. I like the comfortable ease she's fallen into at my apartment, like she's been here before and this isn't something new. My apartment is a far cry from Elle's West Hollywood penthouse, but you'd never know by how comfortable she's made herself.

"Promise me something, will you, Elle?"

"Promise you what?" she asks. Her voice is tight with something that sounds like concern. I brush my knuckles over the soft curve of her cheekbone and press a quick kiss to her temple, trying to ease whatever she fears I'm about to say.

"That we'll repeat last night again tonight . . . the bedroom part." I chuckle, and she sinks closer against me. "Maybe tomorrow night, too."

She releases a sigh and tips her head back with a soft laugh. "I think that can be arranged." She leans up and brushes her lips against mine just as the doorbell rings with our dinner.

seventeen

Elle

The showerhead in my apartment squealed as I shut it off, and I blindly reached out to grab the fluffy towel from the hook. Within the confines of the white marble, I quickly dried off, knowing I had to get out of there before Kas made it back from getting a few more things from his apartment.

Yeah.

He was back.

Back in a big way.

So maybe our relationship started off in an unorthodox way. But that didn't mean it wasn't real.

And I was sure it was.

Sure when he looked at me like I was *his* princess. That he really wanted me for me. And when he reached for me in the middle of the night, stealing my breath as he'd slide into me, that he was really loving me.

It made it all the more pathetic that I was sneaking out to have dinner at my parents without telling him where I was going.

Not cool.

I knew it.

Of course, I did.

The truth was, I needed to work a few things out in my heart and mind.

I wasn't quite ready to tell him who my father was. Not yet.

One day, and soon, I would be.

But I felt as if I owed it to my parents to set it straight about the real reason I hadn't shown up my daddy's premiere three weeks ago. I'd given then nothing more than a lame excuse that I knew they hadn't bought. Now, I needed to tell them the reservations I'd felt when I'd first met Kas and truth of his promises.

Then Kas and I needed to sit and have a talk.

A real deep talk like the ones he'd tried to coax me into when he'd first moved into my apartment.

I was going to tell him about Christopher. Tell him how he'd used me to get close to my dad, willing to sleep his way to the top. Even if that meant sleeping with the director's daughter.

That man had stomped all over me on his climb to the stars. He'd left me scarred and scared. But I wasn't broken. Not even close. And I was going to prove that to Kas.

I just had to make it through this dinner first. Admittedly, my daddy wasn't going to be all that enthused when he found out an aspiring actor/insanely sexy underwear model was my new roommate/boyfriend.

Yeah.

That wasn't going to go over all that well.

Sucking in a breath, I quickly dressed, pulling on the most modest blouse I owned.

Brownie points.

Yep, I was totally going to have to sweet talk my way through this one.

I dried my hair and swiped some clear gloss over my lips before smacking them in the mirror.

Ready.

I grabbed my purse and headed for the door.

I fumbled in my tracks when it swung open two seconds before I got to it.

"Hey, Princess," Kas said, a cocky smirk climbed onto his mouth when he saw me standing there. I was basically panting as

I stared at him and wondered how the hell I was going to get out of this one.

"Couldn't even wait for me to get through the door before you were running to me," he muttered so roughly that I was sure the barely there scruff on his jaw was raking my skin.

Right inside the door, he ripped his tee over his head.

Holy Mother Mary.

The man had it all wrong, but oh so right.

My mouth went dry.

Kassius was a sculpture. Pure muscle that shouldn't have been real. Carved and chiseled and gleaming like a million-dollar piece of fine art.

No wonder Calvin Klein was paying him so much money.

Everyone wanted a little piece of that.

But this boy was mine.

I almost said screw it and came up with another pathetic excuse to tell my parents why I wouldn't be able to make it for dinner. But I hadn't seen either of them since I missed the premiere, and I was pretty sure they would be banging down my door to make sure I was okay if I didn't show tonight.

Kas frowned. "What's going on?"

"Uh . . . um . . ."

My eyes darted to the door behind him, and I wondered whether I could make a clean getaway if I ran fast enough.

That wouldn't be suspicious at all now, would it?

"Um . . . you remember my friend I told you about? Kaylee? She texted and wanted to meet up for a drink. We have a lot to catch up on. *A lot*," I overly enthused.

"The one who just started dating Paxton Myles?"

I gulped. "Yep, that's the one. I was going to text you to let you know I'd be gone for a few hours and that I'd meet you back here later."

His eyes narrowed just a bit. "Then why are you sweating?"

Crap, was I?

My fingertips fluttered across my brow, swiping away the moisture. "Sweating? Who me? I'm not sweating."

God, I was rambling like a moron.

He took a step forward, his head angling to the side, his grin growing. "I think you're lying to me."

He didn't seem angry.

Just a little . . . confused. Maybe even amused.

Apparently, I was that bad of a liar. Go me.

I fidgeted. "Okay, fine. I'm going to dinner at my parents' house."

"Scandalous," he tossed out.

Right.

Why did I feel like I had to keep it from him again?

Oh, yeah, I hadn't let him in on the fact my father was Roger Ward. *The* Roger Ward.

"They're a little . . . overbearing."

His brow lifted in speculation. "Overbearing? Don't they live in town? They haven't been by once since I've been here."

"Oh, they were out of the country for a bit."

There I was, digging myself deeper and deeper. I kind of wanted to climb into it and hide.

"I want to meet them."

"NO!" I shouted way too fast, lurching forward.

He jerked back. "No?"

My tongue darted out to wet my lips. "No . . . it's a bad time and . . . and . . . and my mother is a horrible cook."

God. I really was a bumbling idiot.

Before I could make it worse, I ducked around him and made a beeline for the door. "I'll be back later."

I slammed the door shut behind me, resting my back against it as I tried to catch my breath.

Guilt squeezed my ribs.

I hated lying to him.

Hated it, when he had been nothing but honest with me. I just didn't know what else to do. Before I turned back around and confessed it all, I strode to the elevator and rode it to the garage floor. My sandals clacked on the concrete as I rushed for my car, which was parked in the very last spot by the far wall.

I hopped in the driver seat and punched the ignition button, turning my head to the left, only to get caught up on the television attached to the wall near the guard shack.

Distracted.

I guessed some things didn't change.

But how could I not get tripped up on the commercial that came to life on the screen?

The man, the sexiest thing I'd ever seen, wearing nothing but a pair of those tight black underwear, his arms folded over his head, exposing those perfect abs.

Attraction skated through me at seeing the exact same ad that had been on that billboard all those weeks ago.

My boyfriend was a *freaking Calvin Klein model.* Good God, I really was in deep.

Another ad came on, jarring me back into reality. I glanced at the dash.

Crap.

I was going to be late.

Again.

I threw my car into reverse and started to gun the accelerator. Just as quickly, my foot was jamming down the brakes because a hand slammed down on the rear of my car.

Kas was standing there, smack dab behind my car, with both of his hands flat on the trunk. I threw the car back into park and jumped out. "Are you crazy?"

"Are you trying to run me over again?"

"You're the one who jumped behind my car. Seriously, what is wrong with you? Do you have a death wish?"

"Actually, I was kind of hoping not to get my heart broken."

That had me rearing back, eyes narrowing as I stared at him. "What do you mean?"

He roughed a hand over his short crop of dark hair. "Come on, Elle. I might be a model, but that doesn't make me stupid. I know you're lying to me."

A strained sigh left me, and that guilt swelled so high I was sure I was going to drown on it. I swallowed around the huge lump in my throat, staring at the man I knew I had to trust.

I'd be an idiot if I did something that would make him not trust me. "You're right, I was lying to you."

Heartbreak streaked across his face. That should have been enough proof right there. "You're not going to your parents?" he said, as if he were trying to accept the betrayal.

My head shook. "No, I am. I just didn't want to tell you I didn't want you to come with me."

Rejection flashed across his face, and for a second, his eyes slammed closed. "You don't want your parents to meet me."

I blew out a breath. "No, it's the other way around. I didn't want you to meet them."

He frowned. "Are they not cool?"

No. My parents were very, very cool.

I angled my head, making the decision. "Get in the car."

eighteen

Kassius

Elle taps her thumbs against the steering wheel nervously and worries on her bottom lip as she weaves in and out of West Hollywood traffic, and her anxiousness tugs at my heart. She doesn't want me to meet her parents, what in the actual hell? What could be so bad about her parents? Now that I think about it, she doesn't talk much about her family. I know she's an only child, but that's all I know about her family.

I guess I'm about to find out a whole lot more.

"Elle." I sigh, reaching out and pulling her right hand into my left. "Calm down, please."

She glances at me quickly before turning her eyes back to the road and making a sudden and sharp right hand turn off Sunset Boulevard and then zigzagging through the streets of Beverly Hills.

She resumes her thumb tapping and lip biting, and I squeeze her hand tighter in a gesture of reassurance. Reassurance that tonight is going to be just fine. As we move deeper into the neighborhood, the houses become much larger, and her thumb tapping becomes quicker.

"Holy shit!" I didn't mean to blurt out as Elle pulls up to the enormous double gates of a Beverly Hills mansion. "This is your parents' house?" I ask, leaning forward to get a better look out of the windshield and at the gargantuan house sitting before us.

She lets out a long sigh. "It is."

"You grew up in this house?"

She nods and clears her throat. "We moved into it when I was thirteen. Before that, we lived in Malibu." Her voice is sheepish, as if she's embarrassed of her parents' wealth.

Now I'm the one that's nervous. I've never been inside a house like this.

Hell, I've never been within a mile of a house like this. I grew up in a modest three-bedroom rambler and shared a single bathroom with five people until I moved out.

The gates open slowly, and Elle inches the car forward up the long, circular drive. She parks in front of the large double doors and leans back in her seat, resting her head against the headrest.

I reach over and cup her cheek in my palm. "It's going to fine, Elle. I promise. If your parents are anything like you, I'm sure I'll love them." The reassurance earns me a soft smile along with a short nod.

"Let's do this," she says, shaking off her reservations. I meet her at the front of the car and pull her hand into mine as we ascend the large stone stairs that leads to the massive double doors centering the mansion. Large ceramic pots of lush green plants stand at either side of the stairs and only serve to emphasize the size of the staircase.

Just as we approach the top step, one of the doors flings open. "El—" She stops herself mid-word when she sees me with Elle. I've seen her before, but I can't place where. Her eyes meet mine before falling to our interwoven hands, and she raises her hand to her chest in shock. Her fingers fiddle with the charm that hangs from her necklace as she takes in Elle and me.

"Hi mom," Elle musters, dropping her eyes to her feet.

"Pardon my surprise," she says, a giant smiling crawling across her face. "Elle didn't tell me she was bringing a guest."

I reach out to shake to her mother's hand.

"Kas Cowen, and let me apologize. It was a very last-minute decision for me to come with Elle. We should have been more courteous and let you know in advance."

Her thin, bony hand grips mine as the look of shock and surprise finally falls from her face.

"Lindsay Ward," she says before leaning forward and placing a quick kiss on Elle's cheek. "We have more than enough room at the table."

Elle looks at her mom, her eyes widening as if to silently tell her not to pry any further. Mrs. Ward takes a step back, retreating into the house as Elle and I follow.

The large foyer is formal yet surprisingly modern. A large, crystal chandelier hangs over us showing off the stately space.

"It's just been so long since, Elle has brought—"

"Enough, Mom," Elle snaps and shoots her mother a death glare. The room suddenly tense, Mrs. Ward rubs her hands together nervously and plasters on a nervous smile.

"Well then, please join your father in the parlor for some pre-dinner drinks and appetizers." Mrs. Ward extends her arm toward the hallway that leads to a large room at the end of the hall and smiles politely at me as Elle drags me away and down the hall.

Elle releases my hand and exhales loudly. "Sorry about that. She's just so . . ." She hesitates, and I fill in her blank.

"Nice. She's nice, Elle. And polite, and she was excited that you brought me." I nudge her with my shoulder, and she lets out a low grumble.

"You call it nice, I call it nosy. Just wait until dinner. She's going to ask you a million questions that I'm not ready for her to ask you."

"Elle." I stop dead in my tracks, and since I still have ahold of her hand, she's forced to stop as well. She turns to face me, and I place my hands on her shoulders. "She loves you, Princess, and I. . ." I pause, the word love dangling from the tip of my tongue, "We have all the time in the world for me to get to know your family. Just relax. Please. We'll eat and leave. We'll keep tonight totally casual. We'll ease into this."

I brush my thumb over her bottom lip, and she inhales sharply and closes her eyes.

"There's just a lot you don't know—"

"And that's fine. We'll take all of this slow, okay?" I interrupt her.

She opens her eyes and pulls her lips between her teeth before clearing her throat. "Okay." Her voice is quiet, timid, not the Elle I've come to know. But I do know in my gut that this is nothing that I thought it was going to be. I wasn't sure if I was going to be meeting Joan Crawford's character from Mommy Dearest but upon meeting Lindsay Ward, she was the epitome of kind and welcoming. I didn't know what I expected, but Elle had me worried for nothing.

"Your mother is amazing," I tell her. "You remind me a lot of her." She rolls her eyes and smiles. "So, unless your dad is as ridiculous as Al Bundy, I think we're going to get along just fine."

"I hope so," she says as we walk into the parlor, and I take in all the people sipping their drinks and conversing.

"Ellie!" A deep voice rumbles.

"Hi, Daddy," Elle responds dropping my hand and falling into the arms of a large man.

It's then I realize that the man Elle calls "Daddy" is none other than Roger Ward.

The. Roger. Ward.

Holy shit.

"So, how did you two meet?" Mrs. Ward asks just as I shove a piece of chicken into my mouth, leaving Elle to answer the question. She looks up from her plate and around the large table to find that most of the other guests are lost in their own conversations.

"Umm." She sets her fork down and takes a quick sip of her white wine. "I ran into him over in West Hollywood."

"Literally," I mumble under my breath, and Elle kicks me under the table. Mrs. Ward looks confused at the commotion but doesn't press Elle for further explanation.

"You look so familiar, Kas. Have we met before?" Mr. Ward asks from the other side of Mrs. Ward. I've seen Roger Ward at least a half-dozen times in the last year, the last of which was at the Golden Globes a few days ago, but we've never formally met.

Elle looks at me nervously, and I shake my head from side-to-side. She doesn't know that I know who her father is.

"We haven't," I tell him honestly, and reach for my own glass of wine to swallow down my discomfort.

"You've got one of those faces"—he waves his hand through the air—"and I meet so damn many people, I can't keep them all straight."

"How is work, honey?" Mrs. Ward asks Elle turning the attention back to her.

Elle visibly relaxes and sits back in her chair. "It's good. We landed a new boutique hotel chain and an upscale nationwide grocer. We're going to be insanely busy, but business is going really, really well." Her face lights up when she talks about her career, and I'm incredibly proud of her.

I'm also impressed that Roger Ward's daughter, my Elle, has her own career, her own life, outside of his.

Most Hollywood children live off trust funds and make headlines for their bad behavior, but not Elle. This doesn't surprise me. Nothing about Elle surprises me.

She's every anomaly to typical Hollywood, maybe that's why she's kept her family, particularly her father, a secret from me.

nineteen

Elle

I couldn't stop glancing at Kas where he was sitting at my family's dining table. Calm and composed in all that outrageous gorgeousness that twisted my belly into a thousand knots at seeing him there. At the fact I'd brought him there.

He chatted with my father as if they were complete strangers but could be the best of friends. That was Kas's way. He could charm the pants off about anyone.

God knew that he'd charmed them right off me.

The part that got me the most was he hadn't told my father or mother who he was—that he'd just landed a huge modeling contract and his aspirations went so much higher than that. It was then that I knew without a doubt that he wasn't there to use me to climb to those heights.

I knew that because there was just no way that he didn't recognize my father.

This was Hollywood, for God's sake.

Any aspiring actor would recognize him in a heartbeat.

It was the reason I'd been stalling for so long. But seeing him sitting there, so cautiously causal, as if he got that there had been a reason that I'd kept him in the dark about who my parents were?

It meant the world to me.

More than he could ever know.

I could feel the weight of it scraping from my consciousness, pulling free, the tethers that had kept all those walls around my heart stretching so tight were seconds from snapping and floating away.

I'd come to know Kas Cowen, and he was so different from what I'd ever expected. Him sitting there, laughing at something my mother said, his concern for me as he slid his attention my way with a soft, understanding smile.

I thought maybe I'd never known anyone better.

Or maybe it was just that he knew me better than anyone.

I smiled back at him. Tender in a way I hadn't given him before, no longer questioning his intentions.

I wanted this.

I was ready to let him in. Get over all that heartbreak that had held me back for so long.

He squeezed my knee under the table and then set a gentle kiss on my temple.

From across the table, my mother sighed. I wanted to roll my eyes at her, but with Kas Cowen?

God knew, I was swooning, too.

"Oh, my God, that is one gorgeous man, Elle Ward." My mother grabbed me by the arm and hauled me into a dark corner in the hall. "Why in the world have you been keeping that a secret?"

I looked up at the smile on her face. The thing was? Her eyes were filled with worry.

A heavy guest of air blew from between my lips. "You know why."

She frowned and touched the side of my face. "Is this because of that piece of crap who broke my baby's heart?"

Wasn't it always?

But I didn't want that asshole to have control of me anymore, so I found myself nodding. "Yeah. I just . . ." I looked out into the darkened sitting room before I turned my attention back to her. "I just didn't want to ever let that happen again."

She ran her thumb along the hollow of my eye. "None of us want to be hurt, but being loved makes the risk worth it."

"Is it?"

She angled her head. "Of course, it is. Love is scary, Elle. Terrifying, really. When I met your father, he had all these dreams, and I was scared he was going to put all of those in front of me to chase after them. I almost didn't show up at our wedding because of it."

Surprise had me jarring back. "What?"

"It's the truth. I got cold feet. Of course, because it's your father, he came running right after me and swept me from them . . . carried me right down to the alter. He told me none of his dreams were worth it if he wasn't chasing after them with me."

Affection pulsed and spun. "He loves you like crazy."

Mom gently pushed her fingers through the lock of hair at the side of my face. "I'm thinking that man out there might just feel the same about you."

Old hurt bottled up in my chest, full and tight, and God, I was so ready to let it go. "He wants to be an actor."

She let loose a soft laugh. "I know."

My brows lifted. "You do?"

"Um . . . hello . . . I live in Hollywood and I'm not blind. That man is plastered everywhere. Did you really think you could bring him here and I wouldn't recognize that face? Or that body? Hello, abs. Goodness, Elle, I don't know how you left the house," she teased.

"Mom," I rushed out in a hiss.

"What?" She shrugged as if it were completely normal for her to be talking about my sex life with my ridiculously hot boyfriend.

But I guessed if the rest of the world was going to do it, I was going to have to get used it.

Light laughter rippled from her chest. "Do you think I didn't notice the way he was looking at you? The only thing I'm saying is I get why you're willing to take the risk. For him. With him. Just . . . know this industry can be cruel."

"I know that firsthand," I told her.

Regret passed across her face. "I know you do, and I hate that I let that happen."

"It wasn't your fault."

She gave a slight nod. "I know . . . but that doesn't mean our life didn't set you up to be taken advantage of. Just be ready for what people will say. That there will be people who try to destroy you for no reason other than the chance to get to watch someone suffer. People can be cruel and horrible. Remember, they aren't the ones who count. The main thing is *knowing* him. Making sure you can *trust* him, and when you do, trust him all the way. Don't let people or this town get in the way of that."

My eyes glanced out into the hall where I heard the rumble of my father's deep laughter and the sexy roughness of Kas's voice.

I looked back at my mother. "And do you think I can? Trust him?"

She brushed her thumb across my cheek. "That's something you have to decide for yourself. But I think just the fact that you brought him here might give you the answer to that."

Rustling echoed from out in the hall.

I stepped that direction to find Kas grinning at me. "Are you ready?"

"Yeah."

We said our goodbyes, climbed into my car, and headed back down the drive. I was so happy I didn't even care when a pap in a car on the other side of the street snapped a picture of us.

"Where are we going?"

So what if it was a squeal of excitement that came out behind it. I was excited. I was excited that I was here with Kas. This way. That he'd been looking at me the way he had the whole ride home from my parents'. That he'd jumped out the second I'd parked and ran around to my side, hand taking mine as if he were just as excited as I was.

"Don't you trust me, Princess?" He sent me one of those

smirks from over his shoulder as he hauled me across the basement parking garage. My pulse spiked when I realized where he was headed.

"On that? Um . . . no." I glared at his motorcycle like the death trap it was. "There is no way I'm getting on that thing. Things didn't turn out too great the last time I touched it."

Okay, okay, backed into it.

Same thing.

Kas just grinned, but there was something different about it. Softer and sweeter. His big hand came out to brush along my jaw. "Oh, I'd say it turned out just fine, wouldn't you?"

I trembled.

So maybe I really, really did love his bike.

But still . . .

I turned my attention to the massive hunk of gleaming metal and intimidating leather.

Did he really expect me to get on that?

"I haven't gotten to give my baby any loving since she was so brutally mangled a few weeks ago."

"But your ankle—"

"Is totally fine," he cut in.

A sigh pushed from between my lips.

"Don't break my heart, Princess. I want to show you something." It was all tease and a lure.

How was I supposed to resist him? Apparently, that was impossible, because there I was, letting him place a helmet onto my head as if he'd been preparing for this moment all along. Then I was climbing onto the back of his bike and wrapping my arms around the most gorgeous man on Earth, my chest pushing back tight against all the strength of his back.

Uh.

Yeah.

I guessed I really did love his bike, after all.

Night pressed all around us, Kas took to the streets, though at a much slower pace than I'd expected him to. It felt as if he were being careful.

Careful with me.

ONE WILD RIDE

Street lamps blinked down on all sides, and we rode up the winding road, hugging the curves as we climbed higher, the cool wind whipping on our faces and the darkness holding us like a blanket.

I was wrapped so tightly around his body that I didn't know where I ended and he began, our hearts beating in time and our worlds coming together.

That was what it felt like.

As if we'd stepped into a new realm that was just our own.

Or maybe the reality was I'd just finally invited him into my life.

Showing him who I was and where I came from. No doubt, it was time to share all of it with him all. Give him the reasons I'd treated him with suspicion from the get go.

Guilt climbed into my chest because I knew I'd treated him unfairly.

Judged him without giving him the chance.

What kind of person did that make me?

It felt as if no time had passed at all when he pulled off onto the shoulder, which extended all the way out to an overlook of the rambling city below. Blinking lights going on forever. The city so alive beneath us where it felt as if we'd been elevated to watch over it all.

Kas unbuckled the loop on the helmet and gingerly pulled it off my head. The cool air blowing through my hair sent a shiver across my flesh.

Or maybe it was just the way he was looking at me, his face all lit up in the moonlight that poured down from above.

"You are so gorgeous, Elle Ward."

I smirked at him, though, it was filled with affection. "I'm pretty sure we know who that title belongs to, Mr. Calvin Klein Model."

He brushed his lips across mine. "Your Calvin Klein model."

"Is that so?" I whispered at his soft lips.

"Mm-hmm," he mumbled back, kissing me right there alongside the road. I shifted back when a car blew by, and Kas's laughter rang through the open air.

He stepped back and wound my fingers through his. "This way."

He started for a trail flanked by bushes.

"Where are we going?"

He quirked a brow at me. "I thought we established you could trust me?"

"Well, I guess you didn't kill me on that thing."

"That thing?" he said in feigned offense. "First rule of this relationship? You're going to have to learn not to talk crap about my baby. You'll hurt her feelings."

"Is that so?"

"Yup. You already tried to take her clean out. You're going to have to give her all kinds of love to make it up to her."

"And how am I going to manage that?" Laughter filled my voice.

He gasped as if it should have been obvious. "Riding on the back of her for the rest of your life. That's how."

Love spread through my chest, taking up the guilt I was feeling before. "Why's that sound like an invitation?"

"Because that's what it is."

Continuing to walk toward the edge of the cliff, he angled through the shrubs where bugs trilled in the branches, careful as he led me down the path.

I followed close behind, my sandals slipping in the loose dirt, Kas there to keep me balanced the entire way.

"Funny how roles change, isn't it?" He grinned. "A few weeks ago, it was you who was helping me stand."

It didn't matter that there nothing but cockiness in his words. There was no missing the undercurrent in them. Their meaning bigger. More powerful.

Old reservations churned, vying to make their way up into the broken pieces of my heart.

I pushed them back down.

I was just . . . going to go with it.

Full steam. All the way.

"That's how relationships work, isn't it?" I said. "Give and take. Take and give. It has to go both ways.

We cleared the line of bushes and came out on the other side where the view was one hundred percent unobscured, nothing but city lights spread out below us. The freeways seemed to go on forever, the buildings sprawling out farther and farther until they disappeared at the edge of the night sky.

Kas spun around.

God.

He stole my breath.

Standing there under the moon, his shoulders so wide, the tee stretched across his chest making my mouth water, so big where he stood in front of the city as if one day all of it might belong to him.

"Yeah, Princess. That's exactly how it works." He looked out over the view, his voice drifting far when he began to speak. "The first day I got to L.A., I came up here. I just . . . wanted to look out at what I was going to need to tackle. Put how big it really was into perspective."

He looked back at me. "It's funny how your rationale can tell you it's impossible. There was a huge part of me that screamed to pack all my shit back up, tuck my tail, and head home. Then there was the other part of me that called out that this was where I belonged."

His stare was back on me. Intense. Sincere. "Guess I shouldn't be all that surprised since this is where you are."

"Kas," I whispered.

He cleared his throat. "Seems there are some things we need to talk about." He tugged me down to the earth to side beside him.

Sucking in a stealing breath, I settled down right in front of him. "It seems there is."

He sat with his knees bent, forearms on his knees. He reached down and pinched some dirt between his thumb and index finger. He rolled it around before he finally asked, "Roger Ward, huh?"

"Daddy to me."

A light chuckle rumbled free. "And you didn't want me to know." It wasn't a question, he just turned his penetrating gaze my direction. "Why do I get the feeling there's a story behind this that I should know?"

My heart fluttered in my chest. "I met Christopher at a dinner party with some friends." Finding courage, I pressed on, unwilling to stop once I was finally letting it out. "Attractive. Charming. His entire personality filled up the room." I looked over at him. "Kind of like you."

Anger darkened his eyes. "Now I'm getting the feeling that I'm not going to like this story."

Humorless laughter rippled from me. "I don't like it so much myself."

I looked out over the endless expanse of lights that twinkled below. "He acted like I was the most interesting thing in the world. Like he couldn't be without me. In the end, the only thing he wanted was a way to get close to my dad. To get noticed. He used me as a stepping stool to climb his way into fame. The second he landed an A-list role, he kicked me to the curb. I was nothing to him other than a rung to get closer to what he wanted."

Kas's hands twisted into fists. "Tell me we aren't talking about Christopher Riley?"

The only thing I could manage was a tight nod.

"That piece of shit. I always knew he was a slimy bastard."

I attempted a laugh. "I wish I would have known. It would have saved me a lot of heartache."

Kas swiveled his gaze my way, his tone going deep. "And you were scared that I would do the same? Was that why you didn't want to get close to me? Why you didn't want me to know who your father is?"

Another nod. This one filled with guilt. My eyes pressed closed, and I whispered, "I'm sorry."

A shock of energy blasted through me when I felt the hand come to my face, soft but sure. "Don't apologize for that asshole. I'm just sorry anyone could treat you that way. And I want you to know that I never, ever would. Not ever."

He looked back over the city. "This dream isn't worth it if I'm not living it with you."

"Kas." It was a whimper. Everything pouring out. Gratitude and love and surprise. Because when I'd backed into him, I'd never, ever expected this.

He smiled, didn't say anything when he helped me stand and led me back to the road and carefully put the helmet back onto my head. We rode back down the winding road, this time something different between us.

Or rather, something missing.

My walls gone.

Tumbled to the ground.

I no longer was afraid.

He drove the short distance back to my building, his actions slow and measured when he helped me from his bike and again removed the helmet, his fingers sliding into my hair to fix the mess, or maybe just to mess it up more, because he was tightening his hold and kissing me.

Pushing me against the brick wall.

Stealing my breath.

Two seconds later, we were in the elevator, and he was kissing me deeper.

Passion boiling free.

His mouth and lips and tongue so sweet.

Dizzying.

He swept me into his arms at my door, and a yelp of surprise blistered free. "Kas . . . your ankle."

He shook his head. "This what a relationship is, Elle, remember? Taking turns holding up the other when they need it. And right now, you need me to hold you. And God, maybe it's me who just needs to hold you, too."

He carried me into my condo, his steps strong, but a hint of his limp was still there, and I knew it was probably hurting him. He only held me tighter.

A giggle rippled free when he tossed me onto my bed, one of those smirks riding his mouth. "As much as I like you on the back of my bike, I'm pretty sure I like you sprawled out on this bed even more."

Another giggle, and my hands were pressing to my belly where need was gathering fast. "I like being on the back of your bike."

He set a knee onto the bed and ran his nose up the side of my neck, inhaling as he went. A shiver rolled. "I want you always riding with me. It's going to be a wild one, Elle, this ride. Unforgettable. You and me."

Emotion pulsed at my ribs, so heavy that it had me reaching for him, tugging him up over me, ripping his shirt over his head at the same time.

"Someone's anxious."

"I wanted you the second I saw you. Now I know that you're exactly what I need."

"I should have known I was looking at my future . . . at my life . . . when I opened my eyes and saw you staring down at me."

Kas sat up on his knees, twisted out of his jeans, then leaned down to unbutton my blouse. He pushed it over my shoulders before he peeled off of my pants. I sank back against the bed, feeling exactly like I was a princess when he looked down at me. "You are the most beautiful thing I've ever seen."

I reached up, my fingers running across his chest and down his chiseled abs. They shook beneath my touch, his cock hard and big where it pressed from his underwear. "I'm looking at it right now."

"It's settled then," he said. Then one of those smirks grew on his gorgeous face as he shoved down his underwear. My heart going haywire as he slipped mine down my legs, tossed the scrap of fabric onto the floor, and made a place for himself between my thighs.

"What's that?" I whispered into the night.

The man all lit up in the lights that burned in from the city.

Already the brightest star.

"It's just you and me, Elle. You and me. Forever. You're my life now. Let me be yours. We'll take it on together."

"How could I ever say no to that? Not when I love you the way I do."

The softest smile played around his mouth, and he was pressing into me. So big, he was the only thing I could feel, stealing my breath the same way he'd stole right into my life.

He grunted in pleasure as he filled me full, and then he was wrapping that big body around me, curling his arm over my head as he began to rock. Passion blistered between us, his movements slow, his love intense.

"I love you, Elle Ward. I love all of you."

And he made love to me. Our bodies in sync. Our moans soft, captured in our kisses like treasures. I'd hold on to them forever.

I cried out when an orgasm rolled through my body, the intensity of it shattering something inside me. The last chip gone. Kas chasing all the old hurt away.

He followed, his shoulders curling as his muscles bunched, as his forehead dropped to mine, as his body pulsed and throbbed and shook.

I'd never felt closer to anyone, not in all my life. I didn't want to let go, and I got that he didn't want to, either, because when he pulled out, he just rolled me onto my side and wrapped me up from behind.

His breaths panted and his heart pounding.

He squeezed me tight, and I could feel his smile at the back of my neck. "You really are trying to kill me, aren't you, Princess?"

I bit back the laughter, though, the smile that took to my face was impossible to contain. I nestled deeper into his hold. "You kill me, in the best of ways."

His hand smoothed down my belly and he tucked himself tight against my bottom. "Plan on it. Every. Fucking. Day."

twenty

Elle

Sunlight poured in through the bank of windows and basked the bed in a pool of warm, morning light. I stirred against it, stretching beneath the sheets, so deliciously spent I couldn't stop the huge smile from spreading to my face.

I reached out, feeling beside me, only to grin wider when I realized I could hear the shower running from the attached bathroom.

Instantly, my mind was back to last night to when Kas had taken me again and again. Hard and rough and slow and languid and everything between. Every time we'd drift off, he'd be reaching for me again, filling my heart and my soul with whispers of adoration. Telling me over and over how much he loved me. Dreaming about how our lives were going to be.

My spirit drummed.

I couldn't wait.

A vibration stole my attention. I shifted so I could look up behind me to the nightstand on Kas's side of the bed where his phone was going off with a text.

Kas's side of the bed.

I nearly squealed.

Was this real? The satisfied ache throbbing between my thighs promised it was really, really real. Oh, the things that man had done to me.

I rolled around in the covers, hugging them to my chest, pressing them to my nose. Just relishing in the promise.

The promise of forever.

His phone vibrated again.

Bliss streaked through my body as I rolled over, figuring I'd grab it and take it to him in the shower considering whoever it was must need to get in touch with him since it kept going off.

The text preview flashed across the top, and I wasn't trying to be nosy, but there was no missing the name the text had contained.

Roger Ward.

Brow furrowing, I sat up on the side of the bed, hand shaking as I reached out when yet another text came through. I felt like a nosey jerk for opening the screen, but found I couldn't stop myself.

I clicked into the waiting messages.

Dominic: Holy shit, Cowen, you dog.

Dominic: You told me you'd do anything to make it.

Dominic: But snagging Roger Ward's daughter? Brilliant. Deviant, but brilliant.

Dominic: At least I heard she's hot.

Dominic: It was the in you needed. Script is coming your way today.

Dominic: Don't fuck this up by growing feelings. Remember what we talked about. Live it and you'll own this town.

I didn't realize I was shaking. Shaking and shaking and shaking. Unable to see through the blanket of tears that poured down my face as I stared at the words.

Don't fuck this up by growing feelings.

How could he do this to me? After everything? After everything I shared with him? After everything he'd told me last night?

I could feel all the healed pieces inside me splintering. Cracking under the weight. Devastation and hurt and betrayal.

I should have known. I should have known.

But I had. I was the fool who just hadn't listened.

Knowing it didn't mean it hurt any less.

Because I could feel it ripping through me.

Agony.

Torment.

The pieces he'd brought to life in my completely crushed.

And I swore I could hear his voice, calling out to me, could feel the blaze of his touch on my skin.

"Elle!"

"Elle!"

Finally, my eyes snapped up. Kas was there, both hands on my shoulders as he shook me, trying to break through the torment that filled my eyes.

Which was such bullshit.

Such bullshit.

As if he didn't know why.

His phone was clutched in my hand, and I jolted to standing, still clinging to the sheet as if it might protect me from what he did.

He stumbled back, nothing but a towel wrapped around his stupid-hot body.

"How could you?" I seethed.

Kas blinked, panic flooding from his mouth. "What are you talking about? What is going on?" His eyes darted between my face and his phone. "Why do you have my phone?"

Busted, asshole.

"I thought we *shared* everything?" I taunted, wishing it came out hard instead of coated in tears.

In heartbreak.

Because that was what he'd done.

He'd broken my heart.

"We do," he stammered. "What's going on? Just tell me."

I held out the phone. "I trusted you." It was a pained gasp.

Kas grabbed the phone, his face falling when he read what was on the screen. "Elle . . . baby . . . this is my idiot agent. He doesn't have a clue what he's talking about."

Disbelief huffed from my lungs. "Don't . . . just don't. Pack your things and get out."

Kas took a lurching step forward. "No, Elle . . . no, listen to me. He doesn't know anything. He didn't know we were together. He's just making assumptions."

I squeezed my eyes closed to protect myself from his lies.

He reached for me.

Singeing me with his touch.

I couldn't. I couldn't.

"Get out!" I screamed. "Get out! I can't believe I trusted you. You're just like every other asshole in this city. I can't believe I fell for it, but you can bet I won't ever again. Now get out!"

Pain streaked across his features.

No.

I was just another stupid girl getting playing by an actor.

"Elle," he whispered quietly. "I love you."

My eyes squeezed tighter. "Go."

twenty-one
Kassius

What the fuck just happened? I run my hand over my face as Elle slams the door behind me, and the sound of her sobs coming from the other side of it? It guts me.

"Elle, please!" I plead with her through the barrier between us.

"I said, go away!" Her voice trembles through her sobs.

"Talk to me, Elle. Let me explain."

"There's nothing to explain. I said, go away!"

"Fuck!" I slap her door with my open palm before I turn down the hall and walk to the elevators. I hold my phone, Dom's name flashing across my screen with an incoming call, and I want to break the stupid fucking thing. A stupid misunderstanding because of Dom's fucking idiotic text messages and his shitty humor—a misunderstanding that feels more like an ending now thanks to him.

I punch the button on the key pad to take me to the parking garage and I bang my head back against the elevator wall in frustration. I have no idea how I'm going to make this right, no idea how I explain what a jackass Dom is. Guilt pools in my stomach as I recall the look of hurt on her face. She thinks I betrayed her. Lied to her. Fuck!

ONE **WILD** RIDE

The elevator doors slide open, and I step out into the parking garage on a mission, headed to my bike and straight to Dom's office. Fucker is going to help me make this right if it's the last thing he does for me.

I start my motorcycle and crank the throttle, revving the engine loudly as I take off. I'm angry and being reckless, and as soon as I realize this, I reel it in, both my temper and my careless driving. By the time I get to Dom's office in Burbank, I'm even more on edge. Less than a minute later, I'm busting into the reception area, ignoring his administrative assistant and her warning that he's on a call.

"Not now, Annabelle," I bark at her and push through his office door. "Hang up!" I announce as I slam the door closed behind me and right in Annabelle's face. I'll have to apologize for that, and my outburst, later. Dom shoots me an annoyed look and covers the mouthpiece of his phone, trying to drown out my disruption.

"Let me call you back. Have to deal with a problem that just came up," he says, looking right at me, his eyes narrowed in annoyance.

Dick.

I reach forward and press the *end call* button on his desk phone disconnecting his call before he finishes speaking. His eyes widen in surprise and I lean forward on his desk, both hands safely planted so I don't succumb to the urge to reach across the oversized desk and strangle him.

"What the fuck is your problem?" he barks and pushes himself up from his chair. Dom is smaller in height and lighter in weight than I am. I'd crush him if he came at me, but I wouldn't do that to him. He's been a good friend to me, and an excellent agent, until the texts.

"The texts." It's all I can barely muster, anger raging through me.

"Calm down, Kas. The script is right here." He reaches out and tosses me a bound stack of papers that bounces off my chest and lands on the desk in front of me. "Jesus Christ, Kas. I told you I'd have it to you today. Give me a minute to deal with some of my other clients shit before you come busting in here demanding things from me. That Calvin Klein contract is barely dry, and this is how you're going to act now that you're some hot shot?" He sits back in his desk chair and props one foot over the opposite knee.

Those words sting. I swore I'd never change who I was, and for Dom, my agent, and my one true friend in Hollywood to think that I have, hurts. I drop my head in frustration, the anger seeping from me. "It isn't about the script, Dom. Elle saw your texts. She thinks I'm using her to get to her father."

"So?" He shrugs and rolls his eyes.

"So? That's all you've got to say, so?" I pound my fist against his desk in anger.

"Well, isn't that what you're doing, Kas? I mean you can't be *that* serious about her. She's a no one in Hollywood. I mean, she's Roger Ward's daughter, and a complete babe, but she's a no one in this business. It just makes sense that you'd tap that, get to Ward, and move along."

"Tap that?" I repeat. Rage courses through my veins. I can feel my heart throttle in my chest and heat take over my body. "Don't you ever talk about Elle like that again, do you understand me?" I lean across his desk, almost pressing my face to his, so close that I can see the sweat along his hairline. He leans back, creating some distance, and swallows hard.

"Shit, Kas. I didn't know it was that serious." He rubs his hand down his tie and looks away from me awkwardly.

"Well it is, and you fucked it all up with your fucking text messages."

"Shiiiiit," he hisses and rubs his chin. "I'm sorry, man. I really am."

"She won't even listen to me, she won't let me explain. We finally got to this great place and she admitted to me that she was used in the past by a boyfriend . . . that fucker, Christopher Riley, you know him." Dom rubs a temple and nods as I tell him the story. "She recently told me about him and then woke up and found my phone on the nightstand with your texts on full display. Those texts destroyed her, Dom."

"You know I didn't mean it like that." Dom huffs, swiveling

nervously in his desk chair. "I was just—"

"I knew what you meant, but Elle didn't. She kicked me out, told me she never wanted to talk to me again, that it was over." I pause. "I can't lose her, Dom. I can't. I actually love her."

He looks surprised at my confession. I'm not a fall-in-love kinda guy. "What can I do?"

I push off his desk and pace his large office, stopping to look out the large office windows. "I need to make this right, and I need you to help me."

"How?"

"I don't know yet, but she has to understand that those texts from you are not how I feel."

"Okay, I will help you. But, Kas, I need you to change gears for a minute. You have to read that script, right now. You going to read for the casting agent in four hours."

I snap my head back, turning my attention back to Dom. "What?"

He holds up his hands in defense. "I know that the timing is less than ideal. They called about ten minutes before your entrance, and they want you for this project, Kas. They want you bad, but we have to go through the formalities. You have to read for the casting director and they want to do that this afternoon," he glances at his watch. "They highlighted the pages that they want you to read, so read them, study them, memorize them. Own them."

"I don't know if I can do it," I admit, as my stomach turns. "I've got too much on my mind—"

"It's an emotional scene, Kas. Channel your hurt into this reading. I have complete faith that you can do it. While you're doing that, I'll work on what I can do to make this right with Elle."

"That was exceptional!" the casting director says as she claps her hands wildly. "I really didn't know if you'd be able to pull that off. The intensity of that scene is like none other. I could almost feel your heartbreak and sadness." Blair wipes a stray tear from under her eye. "You have a real gift, Mr. Cowen. To be able to walk in here and read a scene that intense and make me feel it . . ." She puts her hand to her chest over her heart. "You're perfect for this role. Just perfect."

I nod and swallow against my dry throat. If only she knew how heartbroken I truly am, she might understand how easily it is for me to channel it into my reading.

"This is a modern-day Romeo and Juliet. A forbidden love story, and you, young man, have nailed it. You have the looks, the passion, the charisma. Everything is perfect."

"Thank you," I say quietly, wanting to get the hell out of here and over to Elle's.

"We'll be in touch. Until then," she pulls off her glasses and raises an eyebrow, "I'd consider getting started on that script." She points at the papers I hold in my hand, as I shuffle them around. "There will likely be minor changes, but the more you are prepared the easier it will be for you to step into this role. I'm telling you this unofficially of course."

I twist the manuscript in my hand and offer her a tight smile. "Of course. Thank you for taking the time to have me read for you today."

"It was my honor. We'll be in touch . . . soon." She winks and ushers me to the door. As glad as I am to have had this opportunity, my only thoughts are of Elle and how I'm going to make this right.

I park in the garage at her condominium complex and take the elevator up to her floor. Damn near the entire hallway outside her door is lined with vases of roses. I guarantee that was Dom's doing. My heart begins to race as I near her door, juggling the large vase with two dozen roses I brought in my hands. I texted her before I went to my reading, begging her to call me. She hasn't. I just need her to listen to me. To give me five minutes to explain.

I raise my hand and knock rapidly four times. Blood swooshes through my ears as I wait nervously for her to answer. When she doesn't, I knock again and wait. Finally, after knocking a third time, I holler through the door, "I know you're in there, Elle. I saw your car in the garage."

When she still doesn't open the door, I lean forward and press my forehead to cold wood. "Please, Elle, let me explain."

I wait another minute, and then have to choke down my emotions when I hear the click of the deadbolt. My stomach jumps and my heart stills as the door crawls open.

"Kas." The voice is firm and cold. It's Lindsay Ward. Not exactly who I was expecting or hoping to see.

"Mrs. Ward. Is Elle here? I've been trying to get ahold of her."

"I heard." She purses her lips and crosses her arms over her chest before her eyes go wide as she notices all the roses.

"Please. I just need to see her for five minutes."

She holds up a hand and steps toward me. "She isn't here, and even if she were, she wants nothing to do with you."

"Please, Mrs. Ward. This is big misunderstanding. I love her. I *love* Elle. I would do anything for her, and damn it, I'm trying."

"Sounds to me like you're willing to do anything to land a role in major motion picture." Her eyebrows shoot up and she looks at me suspiciously. My heart sinks with those words. I realize nothing I say is going to change what Elle or Mrs. Ward think about me. They're holding on to the pain and anger of what happened before. They think I'm just like him. Using Elle to propel my career.

"I am not Christopher Riley." I snap at her. "I would never use Elle. Or intentionally hurt her. What she saw was a series of shitty texts from my agent. Those texts do not reflect how I feel about her or what I would or would not do for her or my career."

She takes a step back at my outburst and nods. My voice softens, the hurt coming through. "I love her, Mrs. Ward. More than I've loved anything or anyone. She is *it* for me. She is the only thing I want in this entire world. If I have to spend forever proving that to her, I will. I just need her to talk to me." My voice cracks with emotion, and the anger on Mrs. Ward's face dissolves.

She sighs. "I could tell at dinner the other night how smitten you are with her. So, you can imagine my surprise when Elle called me this morning and told me what happened."

"But, It isn't what she—"

Mrs. Ward holds up her hand to stop me.

"Regardless of what she thinks, you need to give her some time to cool down. I know you love her, and, Kas, she loves you, too. That's why this hurts her so damn much. She trusted you, and when she saw those texts, she immediately felt taken advantage of. Give her some space and let me talk to her—"

"How long do I give her?" I cut Mrs. Ward off. "How long do I wait? This is literally killing me. I can't think about anything other than her."

She reaches out and touches my arm. "I don't know, Kas. I just know that she needs some time to think through all this."

"Will you tell her I came by, and that I love her . . . and ask her to please call me?"

"I will."

"And will you give her these?" I hand her the giant vase I've been cradling in my right arm, surprised that I haven't dropped them yet.

She takes the vase of flowers and offers me a tight smile. "Get some rest, Kas. I'll do what I can." I take a hesitant step back and finally turn around to leave only to stop again.

"Mrs. Ward," I call to her.

"Yes, Kas."

"I love her. I really love her."

"I know you do, son. Good night."

twenty-two
Elle

I slumped down at the massive table and buried my face in my hands. In Paxton Myles's kitchen, no less.

One of the most successful, famous actors in the business.

All because my conservative, straitlaced, kindergarten teacher and best friend had hooked up with him the night I'd run over Kas.

Oh, the fates were laughing, weren't they? Hitting Kas had made me miss my father's premiere, and in turn, I'd shoved Kaylee right into Paxton's arms all while I'd fallen at Kas's feet.

Heartbreak burned across my chest.

I tried to fight it, but a tiny, pained moan leaked from between my pursed lips.

I was trying . . . trying so hard to be okay. I wasn't exactly succeeding.

A gentle hand reached out and touched my arm. "Hey, it's going to be okay."

I lifted my head and looked across at Kaylee, who was watching me with sympathy.

"Will it?" I asked.

"You know it will."

"Then why does it feel like it won't?" Sorrow rushed out with the question, this helplessness that made me feel nothing but weak and pathetic.

Her head tilted to the side. "Because you're right in the middle of the storm. Right now, it feels impossible to move on from this point, but you will. No matter which direction you end up heading."

A frown pulled at my brow. "Oh, I think we both know what direction I'm heading."

"And where is that?" she asked, voice wry and somehow sounding like the most soothing thing.

"Straight into a pit of loneliness. You know . . . that hell where lonely spinsters live with their fifteen cats? It's my destiny."

"So dramatic."

"So true," I tried to tease, but it fell flat. The little bit of lightness I'd found slipping away when I offered her the complete truth.

Because that's what it was.

"I'm heartbroken, that's what I am, Kay-Kay."

Tears pricked at my eyes as soon as I let the admission free.

Kas had absolutely broken me. I'd thought Christopher had. But this? This was different. This was a gutting sort of pain that gripped me everywhere, hollowing out something right at the center of my chest, leaving me with a gaping hole. One so vast I wasn't sure it could ever be filled.

Her expression fell, and she reached out and fiddled with some of the hair that had fallen from the haphazard knot I'd tied it into when I pulled myself from bed this afternoon. I hadn't even bothered to brush it. "I'm so sorry you're going through this."

"I can't believe I fell for it again." My chest stretched tight at the realization of what I'd allowed myself to do. At how far and fast I'd fallen.

Questions slid across her face. "Are you sure that's what you did? I know I don't know him, but from everything you told me, this came from out of nowhere."

"Just like it did with Christopher."

"Maybe for you." She hesitated for a beat, as if she didn't want to say it. Remorse filled her voice when she finally said, "I hate to say this, Elle, but I think the rest of us knew what he was up to. There was something about him that always made me question him."

My lips pursed. "You tried to warn me, and I didn't listen."

"I did . . . but sometimes there are just things that people can't tell us, and we have to learn them for ourselves."

Frustration left me on a huff. "You'd think I'd learn the first time."

"Maybe there is a different lesson in this situation," she offered.

My head shook. "I don't think so, Kay. I saw it with my own eyes. It might as well have been written in bright, shiny letters. There was no mistaking their meaning."

Kaylee refilled my glass of red wine, peeking over at me while she did. Taking the glass, I held it between both hands, clinging to it for dear life and took a deep, steeling pull.

I could feel her eyes on me.

The girl was working up to something.

I wasn't sure I was ready to hear whatever that was.

Because it all hurt too bad. I'd finally, finally let myself go. Freeing myself of those chains Christopher had bound me with. Finally trusting and putting my heart out there for someone to hold it.

And not twenty-four hours later, Kas crushed it. Crushed it in a way I had been entirely unprepared for because I don't think I'd been prepared for how much I actually cared about Kas. For how much I loved him. What I'd felt for Christopher had been nothing but a shadow of what I felt for Kas.

Kaylee cleared her throat, dragging me back from the thoughts I was spiraling into, her question cautious but pointed. "But those weren't Kas's words, were they? You were reading someone else's thoughts?"

I gave a furious jerk of my head. "No. It was clearly a conversation. Something they'd discussed before. It was his agent, for crying out loud."

What his ultimate goal was.

Roger Ward.

A shudder ripped through my body, and my heart gave another pained quiver.

The moisture that had gathered in my eyes finally broke free. Hot tears streaked down my face as I choked out the words. "I should have known better than to have taken him to meet my daddy."

Although, I guessed he had probably known who I was, all along. The man playing me this entire time with that body and those teases and the adoring look in his eyes.

It'd been nothing but an act.

Asshole deserved an Academy Award.

"If he really was using you to get to your father, it's better he met him sooner rather than later before you were too wrapped up in him."

"If?" It was a choked accusation. Because I knew the truth. And the truth was that I'd been used, and I was already so wrapped up in him that I didn't know how I was ever going to recover from it.

From losing him in the same damned way.

Dumb girl.

I huffed out a frustrated sigh and buried my face in my hands, head shaking as I groaned. "Why do I always fall for assholes?"

Kaylee reached out and pried my hands from my face. "Because you have a huge heart, Elle. Sometimes falling in love is impossible not to do, and when you do it, you do it hard. He made you feel something, and I'm guessing there was no stopping that. And after everything? The things he told you when he was leaving? I have to wonder if maybe you didn't misunderstand."

My chest tightened, and that sickness in my stomach twisted. "No."

She glanced to the clatter of noise that suddenly came from the back of the house.

Paxton's familiar voice echoed on the floors as he spoke to someone on the phone.

Love lit on her face as she gave a longing look over her shoulder before she looked back at me, leaning in closer. Her expression twisted in a pleading kind of emphasis. "I almost lost my chance with Pax because I didn't give him the chance to explain himself. Because I just *expected* him to hurt me. Because I expected him not to really want me. Because I just expected him to break my heart. Rather than giving him the benefit of the doubt and trusting the man I'd fallen in love with, I made that decision *for* him, and I almost missed out on the love of my life."

Pain lanced through my worked-over spirit. "You got lucky."

She frowned at me. "Yeah, I did. And who's to say it isn't your turn to get lucky?"

I gruffed out a sigh. "The Hollywood Gods, apparently. They hate me."

Kaylee rolled her eyes. "So dramatic. Maybe you should be the actor here."

"Hardly."

Footsteps echoed on the floor, and Paxton appeared in the back doorway, striding into the kitchen. He flashed his signature smile that sent millions of women into a swoon.

Kaylee was no different. She was grinning like a fool when he walked over and pecked a kiss to the side of her head. "Hey, gorgeous," he murmured.

Love radiated from her. "Hey. How was your meeting?"

"Good now that it's over and I get to look at you."

She swatted at him, and the man nuzzled her neck, and she released a tiny squeal as he whispered something in her ear.

I rocked back in my chair and crossed my arms over my chest. Gross.

Kaylee giggled.

Okay. Not gross.

It was kind of adorable, and it made me feel all the worse.

God, what was I going to do with my life?

Kaylee suddenly sobered, hanging on to Paxton's arm that he had wrapped around her shoulders so he could hug her against him. "Sometimes people surprise us, Elle, and it doesn't always have to be in a bad way."

I looked off to the side, out the window to the rambling lawn that fronted the mansion, the wrought iron fence enclosing the space. Finally, I looked back at her. "I don't know how to trust him."

She blinked back at me, sympathy in her eyes. "Maybe start by listening to him."

But it was hard to listen when you'd been hurt so badly that the thought of experiencing it all over again was too much to bear. Too bad it was no longer just a thought.

Because a fool, I'd fallen in love with him. Gave him the power. And with that power, he'd obliterated me.

twenty-three
Kassius

"Bagels," I mumble to myself. It's a brilliant idea. Elle loves those fucking jalapeno bagels and the caramel lattes from that little bagel shop down the street from her condo. I throw on a pair of shorts and a tee as I grab my car keys and wallet, a man on a mission to win his girl back with her favorite breakfast.

She won't say no to bagels and coffee.

My muscles ache as I move quickly to get pulled together and my shoes on. I maybe slept for thirty minutes last night because I was too busy checking my phone and hoping for a response from Elle.

And I got nothing.

Her silence is eating me alive, and I'm a desperate man at this point.

I slide into my old SUV, throwing on my sunglasses as I weave into the LA traffic. Even on a fucking weekend morning, traffic is a bitch in this city. Thankfully, I find a meter right in front of the bagel shop, but the line is out the goddamn door, and every table on the tree-lined West Hollywood sidewalk is taken. I forgot how popular this place is.

I keep my eyes trained low, fidgeting with my phone and hoping no one recognizes me. The line moves quickly, thank fuck, and in only a few minutes, I'm placing an order for three bagels, cream cheese, and two coffees. I know the way to her heart is through her stomach, and I'm praying to all Gods this will work. She *has* to talk to me.

Just as I hand the cashier my card to pay for my order, I hear, "Elle. Your toasted jalapeno bagel with veggie cream cheese and caramel latte is ready!" Coming from a pimply faced teen with a baseball cap and a voice that almost sounds prepubescent.

From across the store, I see Elle's lean body glide up to the counter. She's all beauty, wrapped in yoga pants and tank top with her messy hair held back by her sunglasses propped on top of her head. My heart falls when I see the same exhaustion I have marring her beautiful face.

Tired.

Broken.

Hurt.

Never in my life have I felt what I feel when I see Elle. You can't ignore the intensity between us, and I know she feels it, too. Just like I can sense her hurt, and I can see her pain.

She offers a weak smile to the teenager holding her bagel and coffee, taking them from him carefully. Maybe she can feel the heat of my stare because she glances over her shoulder, her eyes meeting mine as if she knew I was there, silently summoning her.

Her shoulders rise with a sharp inhale when sees me, and she pinches her eyes closed tightly as if doing so will make me disappear. I move frantically, stumbling through the small, crowded space as she turns her back to me. I want to call her name, but my voice is stuck in my throat, and just before I can get to her, she's gone. Exiting through the side door.

My heart physically hurts with her absence.

"Kassius," I hear my name called by the same teen who just gave Elle her breakfast. I give my head a little shake, brushing shoulders to get to the pick-up counter. I reach out to take the bag of bagels and two cups of coffee from the teen. Just before I get to the same side door Elle just slipped out of, I toss the fucking bagels and coffee into the trash can.

Fuck this day.

ONE WILD RIDE

I threw my keys across the apartment, and they land with a loud thud against one of the kitchen cabinets before falling to the floor with a *clank*.

With heartbreak still swirling inside me, I dive onto my sofa, burying my face in an oversized throw pillow. I'm at a loss for what to do to get Elle to speak with me. My eyes burn with tears and my blood pressure rises in frustration.

Elle saw me and she walked away, goddammit! My heart physically hurts at how easily she dismissed me. Like I was nothing, like I meant nothing to her.

My phone rings, and I pull it from my back pocket to find Dom's name flashing on the screen. I ignore the call, sending it to voice mail and then tossing the phone onto the coffee table. I am in no mood to talk to anyone right now.

Not ten seconds later, the damn thing rings a second time.

Again, Dom's name appears in large white letters against the black screen, and again, I hit ignore, only this time I flip the button to silence the phone. I'm about to toss the device away, but pause when another number flashes across the screen.

One I don't recognize.

"Fuck," I grumble, but slide my finger across the screen to answer it. "Yeah," I answer, my voice laced with frustration.

"Kas?" the deep voice asks. "Kas Cowen?"

"Speaking."

The man on the other end of the phone clears his throat. "Roger Ward here."

I sit straight up and inhale a sharp breath. Roger Ward. Elle's father. Jesus Christ he's calling to set me straight. I know how fucked up all of this is, but I need him to understand like Mrs. Ward hopefully does.

"Mr. Ward, please let me explain—"

"Explain what?" He cuts me off. "Explain that you had the best damn reading Blair said she's ever seen? And let me tell you, she doesn't speak highly of anyone in this business. Woman hates damn near everyone, including me. You knocked her damn socks off, kid."

"Ex-excuse me?" I damn near stutter.

"You heard me, son. Blair said you were phenomenal. Hold on, let me read her notes." I hear him shuffling some papers around. "Her exact words were, 'Natural talent. Perfection. Hire him.'"

"Wow." Is all I can barely manager to say. My mind is reeling with this news, which isn't at all what I expected to hear from him. I was sure he was calling because of Elle.

"Wow is right. It would be our honor to have you join us as the lead role in *Pulled.*"

"Umm, I don't know what to say," I stumble around my words. "I mean—"

"Say you'll accept."

My heart pounds wildly, but it also breaks at the same time. I can't do this. I won't do this, because this is what Elle will always associate the demise of our relationship with. This movie and why she thinks I got the part.

"Mr. Ward?"

"Yes, Kas."

"I'm honored. I'm flattered, and I absolutely would love to accept this role—"

"Excellent!" he shouts.

"But I can't." My heart sinks, and my stomach flips. "I won't take this role."

"Excuse me?"

"Sir . . ." I don't know how to explain this to him, and while I'm searching for the words, he cuts in.

"Is this about, Elle?" he asks, his voice abrupt.

My throat tightens at the sound of her name and tears sting the back of my eyes. God, I fucking love her. I do my best to clear the choke of emotions blocking my voice.

"It is. You see, I love her, Mr. Ward. And she thinks I'm using her to get to you." I scramble to get everything I need to say out before he either cuts me off or hangs up on me. "I'd never do that. Never. And if declining this role, a role I'd love to accept, is the only way for her to understand how much I love her, then that's what I'm going to have to do."

He lets out an audible sigh. "Son, Eleanor is stubborn. I love that girl more than I love anything in this world, but when her mind is made up, she won't budge. Lindsay told me all about what happened, and not for a second did I feel like you were using my daughter to get to me. I saw how you tried to pretend you didn't know me at dinner the other night." I nod as he speaks as if he can see me. "And I also saw how much my daughter cares about you . . . and I could also see how much you care for her. Let me talk to her—"

"No!" Now it's my turn to cut him off. "Please don't. Mr. Ward. That will only make this worse. My mind is made up, sir. I need to step away from this role—for Elle. Whether or not she'll speak to me again, I don't know. But I do know that I need her to understand that my feelings for her had nothing to do with this role, or anything to do with this business."

"Don't jump to any decisions just—"

"It's final," I say, my voice sharp. "I can't accept your offer. Thank you for the opportunity to audition, and I know you'll find someone equally as talented to fill this role." I feel ill as I say these words to him. This is a dream role, one I've wanted all my life—but it isn't worth it if Elle thinks I used her. "I wish you the best, Mr. Ward, and I hope that someday I'll get the opportunity to work with you, but now is not that time."

An awkward silence fills the phone line, and I can hear him shuffling around.

"Understood." Is all he says in response. "I wish you well, Kas." And with that the line goes dead. Before Dom has a chance to call me, I send him a short text.

Me: Ward offered me the role. I declined.

He responds immediately.

Dominic: You did what? Call me now.

At the sight of his response, I power down my phone and throw it across the room where it lands next to my damn car keys.

I lie on the couch and swallow the bitter taste of defeat. I've lost everything—and by everything, I mean Elle.

twenty-four
Elle

Sitting at my desk in my office, I typed furiously at my laptop. Rays of light streaked through the window that overlooks the city. My view here was almost as good as the one in my condo. Both my corner office and my job were something I was incredibly proud of. Something that was one hundred percent me and my hard work.

Well, that and the encouragement and support my parents had always given me.

But this? My position? I'd achieved this without anyone knowing my father's name. Without associating me with the man who had so much influence over the sprawling city that rested below my apartment.

Working hard and achieving my own personal dreams would always be so incredibly important to me. I cherished my job. I always would. I was proud of it, and I was proud of myself.

But sitting there, the stark reality finally settled all the way to my bones.

Success could never be a replacement for love.

Because I could feel the loss of it all the way to my spirit. A vacancy that glowed inside me. Reminding me how far I'd closed myself off from the rest of the world. And once I'd opened those doors, made myself vulnerable, I could no longer shove all those feelings into the back of a closet to be forgotten like waste.

I pushed out a heavy sigh, squinting my eyes as I focused on rereading the marketing proposal I was working on and not the pain lancinating through my being.

Because I was lonely.

Hurt.

And there was nothing I could do to escape Kassius Cowen. He was everywhere. On billboards and ads, not to mention on the tongue of my assistant who had been in my office twenty minutes ago, waving her *People* magazine in the air and babbling on about the hot new actor who was rumored to be starring in Roger Ward's next movie.

Fuck my life.

My father had tried to call me at least fifteen times in the last two days. I'd ignored his calls. I just couldn't bear to talk to him about Kas. I didn't want him to apologize or explain or reason why he'd had to offer the role to him.

I got it.

Kas was beautiful.

Talented.

A super-star waiting to shine.

The only part of that I couldn't handle was that he'd used me to shoot himself into that stratosphere. That he'd left me behind as he'd shined.

The funny thing was, I loved him so much that there was a really stupid part of me that was happy for him.

Seriously, how fucked up was that?

I pounded on the keys a little harder as if I could beat some of the hurt and frustration out on the computer, ignoring the rumble in my stomach that churned with a sickness that threatened to take me whole.

A light tapping sounded outside my open door. "I'm busy, Clarissa," I said without looking up from my computer.

I just couldn't handle her running in with more details about her newest Hollywood crush.

Crush was right.

That was what I was.

Crushed.

"Too busy for everyone these days, I see."

My father's voice had my fingers freezing on my keyboard and my head flying up, tears immediately coming to my eyes. There was no holding them back any longer. Not when my daddy was standing there in the doorway with his hands shoved in his pockets, looking over at me with so much sympathy and love.

I sat back in my chair, muscles slackened with hopelessness, tears streaking down my face.

"Oh, Elle, sweetheart." He stepped in and moved across my office, rounding my desk, and dropping to a knee in front of me.

That was when I broke. I threw my arms around his neck and let myself weep. His strong arms wrapped around me as he let me cry, gentle words coming from his mouth. The same way as he'd always done when I'd been a little girl, the man filling me with encouragement and belief and promises that everything would be just fine.

Fiercely, I shook my head where my face was buried in his neck. "No, Daddy. It isn't going to be okay. I don't know how I'm going to recover from this one. It hurts too bad."

My shoulders shook with my sobs, and I wasn't sure I was going to be able to stop.

He sighed a sound of affection and leaned back so he could look at me. "Don't tell me you aren't returning my calls because of this Kas boy?" There was almost a tease to his voice.

Nodding, I swiped angrily at my tears. "I can't believe I fell for it again."

Knowing eyes moved over my face. "You've always been incredibly independent."

I blinked at him, not sure what he meant. "That's how you raised me to be. You and mom instilled in me that I could be anyone I wanted to be. That I could always take care of myself."

"And you can. You are so strong. But in the middle of that, I hope you know it's okay to let other people into your life, too. I don't know where I would be without your mother in my life. I know I wouldn't be the man I am now without her. It doesn't matter how hard I worked. She's always helped keep me grounded. Centered. She showed me the kind of man I wanted to be, because God knows, our judgment can get clouded in this world."

"I think I just keep letting in all the wrong people in. God . . ." I looked away, studying a scrap piece of paper on my desk before I finally gathered my courage and looked back at him. "How do we know who to trust, Daddy? I feel like everyone I come into contact with is either judging me or figuring out how they can benefit from me. I hate that feeling . . . like I'm being used every time I turn around. How do you handle it?"

He played with a piece of hair that had fallen free of my twist. "I do my best to surround myself with people who have proven themselves to me. Your mother, most of all. You. Carl and his family. Then . . . the only thing I can do is trust my gut. Listen to my heart. Pay attention. Intentions may not make themselves known right at the start, but they always reveal themselves in the end. I'm vigilant of that. People prove themselves one way or another—trustworthy or dishonest. We just have to make sure we look deep enough to see who people are inside."

Hurt and love billowed through me. Because I'd thought I had. I'd truly believed in Kas. I'd thought he'd proven that he loved me. That look in his eye and the tenderness in his touch.

I'd been so sure.

Maybe it was my own stupid heart that was lying to me.

My dad looked away for a beat, gathering what to say before he looked back at me. "Who did you see when you looked at Kas, Elle?"

Through bleary eyes, I blinked at him. "Honestly? I thought I'd found the man I was going to spend my life with. The one I was going to share my family with."

He gave a slight nod. "Your gut told you? Your heart told you?"

I nodded, unable to speak.

My father patted my knee. "That's good then, because I'm pretty sure Kassius Cowen is the man you believed him to be."

"No, he isn't, Daddy. He used me to get to you," I wheezed, a hiccup of a cry working its way free around the thickness.

He eyed me. "Are you sure about that?"

"He got that big role. He's going to be a star, your name behind him, just like Christopher."

My father rocked back onto his heels, slowly standing, shaking his head as he did. He stared down at me with sympathy and love. "Kas is incredibly talented, and he's bound to make it big in this city. There is no question about that. But he isn't anything like Christopher, Elle."

I stared up at my father. "What do you mean?"

A grin threatened at the corner of his mouth. "I called him and offered him the role. He deserved it. Of every single actor who read, he was the best. Hands down."

Love and pride moved through me. God. What was wrong me? I was actually proud when my father said those words, hopeful for the man who had broken me. I guessed I really was a masochist.

I swallowed down all the hurt and tried to be mature. This was my father's business, after all. "I hope that movie is a huge success, Daddy. Honestly, I do. But I don't think I can handle hearing the details." I pressed my head to my aching chest. "It just hurts too bad."

His lips pursed. "I'm not sure it's going to turn out all that great. Not when the person meant for the role turned it down."

Confusion blistered across my skin, and I could feel the frown pulling at my brow. "What do you mean?"

My dad shoved his hands into his pocket. "Kas was offered the part. He turned it down."

Shock blasted through my consciousness, and I clung to the arms of my office chair as if I were riding a rollercoaster.

That was what it felt like.

As if I were being rocked and flipped and shaken to my core.

My dad took a step back and lifted his chin. "He wouldn't take the role if it meant hurting you."

I sat there, blinking at my skirt as I tried to process what my father had said.

His words spun through my mind as I realized what he'd been trying to say. *The only thing I can do is trust my gut. Listen to my heart. Pay attention. Intentions may not make themselves known right at the start, but they always reveal themselves in the end.*

The same thing as Kaylee had tried to say to me.

Kas was proving himself.

I was the one who'd jumped to conclusions. I was the one who hadn't trusted. I was the one who'd assumed.

In the end, I was the one who'd failed him.

I was the one who'd let him down.

Horror hit me when I realized it was really me who'd done all the breaking.

I flew to my feet.

"Oh my God, Daddy. What did I do?"

My heart was beating fast as I tried to wade through the relief and love and disappointment in myself, tried to catch back up to this reality.

The reality that Kas had been telling me the truth.

That every touch had been real. That every word had been genuine.

He smiled at me. "Nothing that can't be fixed."

"How?" I almost begged.

His grin only grew. "I've got an idea."

twenty-five

Kassius

"Kas, I need you meet me ASAP, as in right now. We have a problem with the Calvin Klein contract," Dom barks into the phone. I let out a sigh and wipe my forehead with a towel. I just finished working out, hoping a long weights session would help me deal with all the shit swirling around in my head.

"Where, your office?"

"No. I'm meeting a client for a late lunch. Can you meet me at the Blue Crescent restaurant off Sunset? I'll be in a private room in the back."

"Give me about an hour. I need to shower quick and traffic will be a bitch."

"I'll be waiting." He then cuts the call.

Thankful to have brought a spare set of clothes with me, I quickly shower at the gym, dress, and then rush out to my car. Easing into traffic, I toggle between radio stations, hoping to keep my mind focused on Dom and whatever is going on with the contract. However, at every goddamn red light, I find myself reaching for my phone to see if Elle has texted me. The answer is always the same: No.

It takes almost every minute of that hour I told Dom it would take me, so I pull into the valet and toss the keys to my shitty SUV at the valet driver. "Take good care of it." I joke as he looks at my car in disbelief. I'm sure he'll park Rodney—that's his name—next to some car that costs more than what both of my parents make in two years. That's L.A. for you. Over the top and pretentious.

I hustle inside, letting the hostess know that I'm here to meet Dom, who's waiting for me in a private room. She escorts me through the tables and down a dark hallway where various semi-private and private dining rooms line the hall, and we stop at the very last one.

I step inside to find Dom sitting at a large round dining table set for eight, his phone pressed to his ear. He nods at me and points to the chair beside him, his way of telling me to take a seat. I round the table and slide into the chair, where a manila envelope with my name scribbled on the front sits on top of the dinner plate.

"Kas," Dom says, ending his call and shoving his cell phone into the pocket of his heavily starched white dress shirt. "Thanks for meeting me."

"What happened to the contract?" I ask, my blood pressure rising. If this contract falls through, I'll vomit. I just can't take any more stress this week.

He reaches for the envelope and sets it in front of him, playing with the little metal clasps as he looks at me. "Well, nothing actually happened with the contract, Kas."

"What do you mean?" I ask, confused. His eyes drop to the envelope and he taps it with his forefinger.

"Well, I brought you here because it seems that there are a few people who would like to talk to you—"

"Me being the first."

I whip my head around to see Elle walking through the door of the private dining room, her eyes fixed on me, looking as beautiful as ever. I inhale a sharp breath when I see Roger Ward follow her through the door.

"And me too," Mr. Ward says. "But I think Elle would like to start." He gestures to her.

My heart races as Elle rounds the table behind Dom and stands next to me. I turn in my chair to get a better look at her, and she reaches for my hand, pulling it into hers. It's soft and she holds it tightly as if I might try to pull away from her.

Never.

"I made a mistake. A terrible mistake," she says, her voice trembling. "Kas, I made an assumption about you—"

"It's my fault," Dom speaks up, cutting Elle off.

"Partially," she says, looking at Dom before fixing her eyes back on me. "But I should have trusted you. I should have given you the opportunity to tell me your side of the story. Instead, I read Dominic's texts and took those as the gospel."

"Elle—" She holds up a hand to stop me.

"I'm sorry. I hope you'll find it in your heart to forgive me after how awful I've been."

I nod, my emotions stuck in my throat. Fifteen minutes ago, I thought I was never going to talk to her again, I thought my contract with Calvin Klein was on the line, and I turned down the biggest opportunity of my life with Roger Ward. Honestly, I couldn't give a shit about the movie or Calvin Klein, but Elle, she is what chokes me up.

"I forgive you." I barely get the three words out.

"Kas, when my dad told me you turned down the role because of me, I was shocked. There is no one in this business that deserves that role more than you. In fact, there's no one else in this business who could walk right into that role and own it. It was made for you." She leans over the table and pulls the manila envelope from Dom's hands. "This right here is the contract you should have signed yesterday when you accepted the role. The part is yours, and I want you to take it." She looks at her dad and then to Dom before turning her attention back to me. "We all want you to take it. It's yours."

I look to Mr. Ward, who has a smile on his face. "Son, yesterday when you turned down the role in *Pulled,* I was devastated. Well, stunned is more like it. No one ever turns down a role in my movies." He chuckles. "But you showed me your integrity, and that is a very rare trait in this business. Now that you and Elle seem to have patched things up—"

My throat is tight and dry. In all my life I've never let my emotions get to me like this, but damn it, if those aren't tears I feel stinging the back of my eyes. I clear my throat and then tip my head back to take a deep, cleansing breath.

I stand and take the envelope from Elle's hand and toss it onto the table. I pull both of her hands into mine, lacing our fingers together. "I will accept the role on one condition."

"What's that?"

I lean in and brush my lips across hers. It doesn't matter that we are in front of Dom and in front of her dad. I don't give a shit. "I'll accept the role as long as I get you."

A giant smile spreads across her face, and tears form in the corners of her eyes. She bites her bottom lip and barely chokes out, "Deal," before I pull her into my arms and plant the longest, most possessive kiss on her lips.

She's mine. As it should be, and I'm never letting her go. Ever.

Roger Ward whistles and Elle pulls back, laughing against my lips. "Let's celebrate," he says, his voice boisterous. "And sign that damn contract, son!"

"I love you," I whisper into Elle's ear before pressing another kiss to her cheek.

"I love you too, Kas."

And in a matter of minutes, my life has fallen back together, and I couldn't be happier. This last week has been nothing short of one wild ride, but it's a ride I'd take over and over as long as I have Elle by my side.

epilogue

"You are so goddamned sexy." The warm voice slipped over me from the side.

A shiver raced down my spine, and I pulled my attention from staring out the window to the man who was sitting beside me.

"Me? Sexy? I hope you looked in the mirror before we left today."

Or turned on the television.

Or scrolled through Facebook.

Or maybe glanced at one of the huge billboards that littered the city we'd just passed through.

Oh, wait, and then there was the bus with his gorgeous face plastered all over the side of it that we'd just passed.

God, the man was the hottest thing I'd ever seen.

And he was mine.

One of those big hands came out to cup my face. "Do you want to know what makes me feel sexy?" He was brushing his thumb along my cheek, and I pretty much lost my train of thought.

"What's that?" I barely got out the breathy whisper.

He leaned in closer, Kas stealing the breath from my lungs when he ran his lips along my jaw. "You . . . standing at my side. That I get to stand at yours. Makes me feel like a fucking king."

Desire rushed me, and I had the urge to climb onto his lap. So

I did. His big body under me as I wrapped my arms around his neck and he wrapped his arms around my waist.

I leaned in, kissing him hard. I wanted to strip him right out of this tux.

Yep, I'd totally forgotten where we were, so much so that when the back door of the limo suddenly swung open I was disoriented.

Lights flashed and people screamed.

Right.

Right.

We'd come to a stop on Hollywood Boulevard in front of the theater.

At Kas's big debut premiere.

The man the star of my father's latest movie.

Oops.

Embarrassed, I pulled back and chewed at my bottom lip while the people crowded behind the ropes on the red carpet cheered and shouted and begged for Kas, desperate to get a glimpse of the man who I couldn't look away from.

Kas cracked a wicked grin, holding me tight on my sides. "As much as I like you on my lap, I think we have an audience."

I couldn't stop the smile from spreading on my face. "I think you always have an audience."

He leaned forward and nuzzled his face in my neck, his voice a rough murmur. "Good thing I only have eyes for you."

I hummed. Body and soul. "And I'll always be your biggest fan."

"Is that so?"

"Mm-hmm."

"Well, we'd better get to it then."

Almost reluctantly, I crawled off his lap, swiveling around and accepting the hand of the driver who was waiting to help me out.

I was wearing a dress that was to die for. Sapphire blue, shimmery and short, a puff of fabric coming off the back to make a train. It made me feel like a queen.

Oh, but the look wasn't even close to being complete without the man who ducked out of the back of the car and pushed to standing at my side.

ONE **WILD** RIDE

The crowd went wild, screams and shouts. You could feel the energy radiating off Kas when he gave me his elbow, as I hooked my arm under it and tucked myself up tight against his gorgeous body.

He owned that red carpet, so perfect where he stopped to chat with reporters, answering questions, posing for pictures.

"It's about time you got here." I whirled around, the biggest smile hitting my face when I saw my best friend Kaylee standing next to her man, the woman both shy and stunning in her red dress. "I thought you were going to ditch me again," she teased.

"Never."

She lifted a brow, a clear *Really?* written on her expression.

I laughed. "Oh, come on Kay-Kay, you totally owe me for that wild night you shared with Paxton. Who knows where you would be right now if I hadn't."

Who knew where I would be.

It was funny how life worked.

How a simple accident had started a chain of events that had change our lives.

Paxton and Kaylee's.

Kas's and mine.

Sometimes it only took one moment to change everything.

An arm looped around my waist from behind as Kas finished answering questions for another reporter who had stopped him. He kissed the back of my neck. Chills flashed. Kas grinned at Kaylee from over my shoulder. "What are you two over here whispering about?"

I glanced up at him. "I was just thinking about the night I met you. It was the same night she met Paxton."

A warm chuckle radiated from his chest. "You mean ran me over."

"It was only a tiny bump," I defended with a teasing smile, which he returned.

"You broke my leg."

"What? I wasn't worth it?" It was all a soft prodding, that feeling inside my chest so full as I sparred with my man.

He tightened his hold. "I'd gladly break every bone in my body if it meant I got to be with you."

Soft laughter fell from my tongue. "I think one broken bone is enough. The last thing I need to do is listen to you whine."

"Hey," he said, all feigned offense and needy hands.

More camera flashes went off.

Yeah, we weren't exactly two who played coy for the camera.

But this was the life.

People knew who we were. We were always under their scrutiny. Their judgment. A part of the news.

But none of that mattered to us. We were just living for us. Not caring what others had to say. The only thing that mattered was that we trusted each other. That every time Kas left, he always came back to me.

We were all finally ushered into the theater. My mother and father were already inside. We went right for them, my mother sending me a secret smile as I approached on Kas's arm, my father holding his arms out to welcome both of us. "There are my stars."

I leaned in and kissed his cheek. "Hey, Daddy. I'm so proud of you. I can't wait to see this on the big screen."

He hugged me tight before he turned his attention on Kas. "It wouldn't be what it is without Kas on the camera. He gave this film life."

Kas shook his head. "It was your direction and vision that made it unforgettable. I'm just honored I got to be the face of it."

We were introduced to Daniel and Melanie Montgomery who were the inspiration of the movie, *Pulled*.

"Kas Cowan . . . it's so nice to meet you." Daniel shook his head.

"The pleasure is all mine. It was quite the experience getting the opportunity to take part in bringing you and your wife's story to the big screen. I can only pray I did it justice."

"I'm sure it's incredible."

He gestured to the gorgeous woman standing at his side. The two of them had to have been in their early forties, their love and devotion for each other so clear in the way they seemed to orbit the other. "This is my beautiful wife, Melanie, although I'm sure she needs no introduction after the role you just played."

Daniel winked at his wife and she blushed.

I pressed my hand to my mouth.

It was adorable.

Kas had talked all during production about their love story, how intense and tragic that it was before they found where their hearts had always belonged.

Kas kissed the back of her hand. I'm pretty sure every woman in a hundred-mile radius swooned. "You are lovelier than the script could ever make you out to be."

"Oh, you really are quite the actor, aren't you?"

"No acting required."

I was introduced, and Kas thanked everyone again, telling them how honored he was to be a part of this project.

It was kind of crazy, how arrogant and cocky Kas could be when it came to me, confident in our attraction and our love. But at the heart of it, he was a humble man. Grateful that he'd found a name in this great big city and cut-throat world.

We found our seats, Kas's hand wrapped in mine. I grinned as Kaylee sat beside me. She leaned in and whispered in my ear. "Did you ever imagine the two of us would be sitting here this way? Both of us tied to two of the biggest names in Hollywood."

"Never."

"It's wild, isn't it?" she mused, shaking her head in awe as she glanced at Paxton, who folded himself into the chair next to her.

"Completely, utterly wild," I agreed, squeezing Kas's hand. He clutched my fingers, holding on tight as my father went to the front and made his introductions, thanking everyone for being there for the premiere.

Then the lights dimmed and the screen came to life.

The first time I saw Kassius Cowen, he'd stopped me in my tracks. It didn't matter that he'd been plastered to a billboard, his arms over his head and his body stretched tight, those abs so delicious in their display that my mouth had watered.

I guessed I should have known I would never be the same when I'd stood staring down at the man on the ground behind my car, the way he'd looked the first time he'd crawled into my bed.

I should have known he was immediately whittling his way into my heart.

But watching him on the big screen was unlike anything I'd ever experienced. The pride that bloomed in my chest . . . for him and my father and for Paxton, who appeared for a smaller role was unreal. All three of them shining with their own incredible talents.

But Kas on the screen? It made my knees weak and my insides quake. My love so intense that I was sure it was going to explode.

Pulse racing, everything hinged on the story that unfolded in these magnificent, unforgettable scenes.

The man was a true star.

So talented I watched wide-eyed. Enraptured and in awe.

He tightened his hold on my hand, as if his own emotion was close to overflowing. Pride and devotion and love coming off him in waves.

His own dreams coming to fruition on the screen.

The credits began to play, and I could barely breathe there was so much emotion clogged at the base of my throat. The lights came on, and Kas looked over at me, eyes glimmering as he studied me. "So . . . what did you think?"

"I think it was brilliant."

"Really?"

"Really. This is what you're supposed to do, Kas. You were made for this."

Just as much as he was made for me.

He grabbed me by both sides of the face and kissed me hard. It was one of those life-altering kisses. The kind that made my head spin and my heart fill so full I was sure it might shatter.

Then he pulled back and stood, stretching his hand out for me. "Come on."

Confused, I took his hand while looking up at him. "Where are we going?"

His eyes gleamed. "I have a surprise for you."

I glanced around at everyone, all who were smiling, my mother and my father, Paxton and Kaylee. All the people who meant the most to us were watching with wide grins on their faces.

There was something in their expressions that made my spirit flutter and churn, butterflies flapping their way to life in my belly, excitement streaking free.

What was going on?

I stumbled along behind Kas as he rushed up the aisle, the man barely nodding at people who called his name, ignoring their requests for interviews and pictures, grinning and saying, "Next time."

"What is going on, Kas? Where are we going?"

I mean, I could rock some heels, but the man was on a mission, and I was basically stumbling along, trying to keep up with him.

He squeezed my hand, one of those cocky grins riding to his sexy mouth. "You'll see."

"Kas . . . it's your big night," I almost begged, wondering what was happening.

"You're right, it is," he said, and then he was stealing my breath again when he stopped outside under the city lights that blinked and flashed all around us, kissing me again, tipping me backward as he did.

Fans shouted and cheered where they remained behind the ropes, and my heart was racing, a thrum in my veins that threatened to make me lightheaded.

He released me, and he swiped his thumb over my bottom lip before he was once again dragging me the rest of the way back down the red carpet.

Only this time, our limo wasn't waiting.

It was his bike sitting at the curb, a driver standing off to the side with two helmets.

The same bike that had changed our lives.

What in the world was happening.

Kas grabbed a helmet and lifted it to help me get it on. "I know you spent about five hours getting your hair done this afternoon. You're going to have to forgive me for messing it up."

Right then, I'd forgive him for anything.

Especially when the man straddled his bike, wearing a tux.

Good God, could anything be sexier than that? Lust swirled and love spun.

I was in so deep.

So deep that I didn't even care I was climbing onto the back in my dress and heels, my senses completely consumed by him as I wrapped my arms around his waist and hugged him tight. He tucked me even closer, a hand over my hands in a show of support, the man waving a hand into the air as what seemed like a blaze of a million blinding flashes went off.

Kas gunned the throttle, winding us onto the road, the night wrapping us whole.

We rode.

People all around us when it felt like the only people who existed was just him and me.

My dress whipped around behind us, and my nerves fluttered free, and the grin plastered to my face had to be the biggest that I had ever worn.

He wound through the city, carefully, though there was something about his ascent as he started up the same hill he'd taken me on the night he'd met my father. Anticipation in each mile that we flew over, the winding of the curvy road spinning us up.

Twining us together.

He pulled off at the same spot as he had before.

Again, he helped me from the bike and unsnapped the helmet from my head.

But tonight, there didn't feel as if there were questions.

We just . . . knew.

I guessed I knew it even more when he took my hand and led me back down the same trail, helping me along the path in my heels, which were definitely going to be ruined.

It was worth it.

Oh, was the man worth it. Every second.

He angled me so we were facing each other, the city nothing less than an endless expanse of glittering lights that blazed with life and opportunity.

"I told you I came up here the first day I got to Hollywood. I wanted to see what it was I was going to have to tackle. All the obstacles that might be laid out in front of me. All that I would have to overcome to reach my dreams."

He touched my face, his hand so soft as he cupped my jaw and tilted my face up to his.

My heart stuttered, the man so stunning I didn't know how I remained standing. A heavy breeze blew through, my hair whipping around us as he stared down at me.

"I knew I would love it here. That I was meant to be here. That I would do everything it took to make it. Little did I know, all those dreams would pale in comparison to my love for you."

Kas dropped to a knee, and I pressed my hand to my mouth as a gasp wretched free and moisture gathered in my eyes. He looked up at me, his tongue darting out to rush across his bottom lip. "You are my dream, Elle. You are this city. You are the screen. You are the words that come from my mouth when I'm acting a scene. You are the epitome of beauty. You are the story of my life."

He dug into his pocket and pulled out a ring. "Live it with me."

Tears streaked down my face, and I threw myself into his arms. "Yes. Oh my God, yes. So much yes."

It was crazy how we never knew what direction we were traveling. When a little bump in the road might change everything.

But I knew I wanted to experience every mile with him.

And I knew it was going to be one wild ride.

the end

Thank you for reading **ONE WILD RIDE**! Did you love getting to know Kassius and Elle? Please consider leaving a review!

More From A.L. Jackson

More From Rebecca Shea

About A.L. Jackson

A.L. Jackson is the New York Times & USA Today Bestselling author of contemporary romance. She writes emotional, sexy, heart-filled stories about boys who usually like to be a little bit bad.

Her bestselling series include THE REGRET SERIES, CLOSER TO YOU, BLEEDING STARS, as well as the newest FIGHT FOR ME novels.

If she's not writing, you can find her hanging out by the pool with her family, sipping cocktails with her friends, or of course with her nose buried in a book.

Be sure not to miss new releases and sales from A.L. Jackson - Sign up to receive her newsletter http://smarturl.it/NewsFromALJackson or text "aljackson" to 33222 to receive short but sweet updates on all the important news.

Connect with A.L. Jackson online:

Page **http://smarturl.it/ALJacksonPage**
Newsletter **http://smarturl.it/NewsFromALJackson**
Angels **http://smarturl.it/AmysAngelsRock**
Amazon **http://smarturl.it/ALJacksonAmzn**
Book Bub **http://smarturl.it/ALJacksonBookbub**
Text "aljackson" to 33222 to receive short but sweet updates on all the important news.

About Rebecca Shea

Rebecca Shea is the USA Today Bestselling author of the Unbreakable series (Unbreakable, Undone, and Unforgiven), the Bound & Broken series (Broken by Lies and Bound by Lies), and Dare Me . She lives in Phoenix, Arizona with her family. From the time Rebecca could read she has had a passion for books. Rebecca spends her days working full-time and her nights writing, bringing stories to life. Born and raised in Minnesota, Rebecca moved to Arizona in 1999 to escape the bitter winters. When not working or writing, she can be found on the sidelines of her sons football games, or watching her daughter at ballet class. Rebecca is fueled by insane amounts of coffee, margaritas, Laffy Taffy (except the banana ones), and happily ever afters.

Connect with Rebecca Shea online:

Page **http://www.facebook.com/rebeccasheaauthor**

Newsletter
https://app.mailerlite.com/webforms/landing/d6b1h4

Rowdy Readers
https://www.facebook.com/groups/527432567356595/

Twitter **http://www.twitter.com/beccasheaauthor**

Instagram **http://www.instagram.com/rebeccasheaauthor**

Email **rebeccasheaauthor@gmail.com**

Printed in Great Britain
by Amazon